OCT 2007
WOODRIDGE PUBLIC LIBRARY
W9-BKE-177
Woodridge Public Library

dry

BARBARA SAPERGIA

Edited by Fred Stenson.
Cover image: *Leaf* by Ligia Botero / Veer (top),
Desert Plants by Gary Hannabarger / Veer (bottom).
Cover and book design by Duncan Campbell.
Printed and bound in Canada by Transcontinental printing.

Library and Archives Canada Cataloguing in Publication

Sapergia, Barbara, date
Dry / Barbara Sapergia.

ISBN 1-55050-319-7

I. Title.

PS8587.A375D79 2005 C813'.54 C2005-904905-7

10 9 8 7 6 5 4 3 2 1

2517 Victoria Avenue
Regina, Saskatchewan
Canada S4P 0T2

Available in Canada & the US from
Fitzhenry & Whiteside
195 Allstate Parkway
Markham, ON, Canada L3R 4T8

The publisher gratefully acknowledges the financial support of its publishing program by: the Saskatchewan Arts Board; the Canada Council for the Arts; the Government of Canada through the Book Publishing Industry Development Program (BPIDP); the City of Regina Arts Commission; the Saskatchewan Cultural Industries Development Fund of Saskatchewan Culture Youth and Recreation; SaskCulture Inc.

Canada Council for the Arts Conseil des Arts du Canada

Regina
CITY OF REGINA

In memory of my sister April,
who loved the land

PROLOGUE

A parcel wrapped in stiff white paper sits on a glass-topped display case brilliantly lit from above. An old man bends over the box. His hair, in loose white filaments to the shoulder, takes fire in the light. He watches as Kuiva, his nimble fingers clasping scissors, snips the doubled cord and splits the wrapping along taped seams, then lifts away paper and cord and drops them to the polished wood floor.

The box, cream-coloured cardboard, bears the label, "J.P. Brancusi, Scientific Supplies and Specimens." Kuiva removes the lid to reveal a host of cleverly nested tetrapacks, each with a cellophane window. The old one's eyes, blue as ultramarine, seem to admonish: Hurry. Hurry, you fool. His hands shake and his mouth works without his knowing.

Kuiva picks up several of the soft paper pyramids, places them on the glass. The old man scans the transparent windows with growing panic. The temperature is right, isn't it? Each pack contains something amorphous, shrivelled, folded in layers like wilted lettuce, vaguely brownish in the pale box.

Kuiva takes a pack, pulls away a thin strip that runs around it, and hands it to the old man. He lifts the top and lets it flutter to the floor. He stares into the pack.

"What have you done? It's not warm enough!"

"The temperature is correct," Kuiva says, "as specified by J.P. Brancusi himself. It may simply take – "

"Be quiet!" the old man orders.

The thing in the box twitches and begins to take a shape, a living thing after all, with a segmented body and two pairs of wings, stretching languidly. And now, just as the company's literature promised, the creature vaults from the box, brushing the old man's hand, and he can't help crying out as it touches his face.

The room is a great circle, its ceiling ten metres above the heads of the two men, dark except for pools of light over the display cases set at intervals throughout. The butterfly climbs the air and passes into darkness.

Kuiva hands the old man another pack, and then another. Each time the same miracle unfolds as the creatures shake off dormancy and rise. The old man stops to watch their flight and Kuiva takes up the opening of boxes, rapidly and efficiently, until a cloud of butterflies rises around them like a column of rushing spirits. Monarchs, brilliant dark-veined orange wings moving in and out of the lights, gold-flecked wing tips flashing. Some circle back to the men, coming to rest on their faces and hands.

"Monarchs are friendly creatures, with little or no fear of humans," Kuiva says. "Brancusi told me that, too."

"Be quiet, I tell you! In fact you can go now."

Kuiva leaves, with dragging steps. The old man doesn't notice.

A butterfly ripples the air at the centre of the room. Light pours from the ceiling to form a bright circle on the floor and music flows through the wide space, a Mozart string quartet, delicate, measured, calm, and infused with longing. A beautiful woman, caught in the light, speaks. "I have always loved you."

The old man draws closer to listen. The butterflies begin to land on him, wings like soft mouths against his face, until his skin disappears under their patterned velvet, only the hard blue chips of his eyes glowing out of the soft mask. The woman's voice floats across the room. "I will never, ever, leave you." Tears leak from the old man's eyes onto the gorgeous wings.

And then the first one dies in front of him, a small orange-brown heap of matter. At first no difference can be seen, there are so many – a lifetime's worth of butterflies in this one great room, flying in and out of the light. So many still on the old one's face. He doesn't notice the second or the third death, but as the minutes pass becomes aware of diminishment, as the creatures collapse in their own minute sectors of space and plummet, their small, soft weight coming to rest on the glowing floor.

PART ONE

1. OVER SOUTHERN SASKATCHEWAN, AUGUST, 2023

Signy's making her rounds. Like a wolf marking its range, only no wolves range as far as she does. The skyboat skims over cracked pavement eroding to friable, slightly toxic new soil. The boat cruises at 120 kilometres per hour, but sometimes Signy likes to slow down and float like a low-lying cloud.

Just for fun, she takes it up to 150 klicks. The sharp stream of air from the window vent flings her hair wildly, cools her face and bare arms. Signy's always loved to go fast, ever since she got her driver's licence. She laughs, thinking of times when the local Mountie pulled her over, but laughing hurts her throat. She stops and watches the land fly by.

The motor shudders, so she lets her speed drop until it sounds smooth again. She definitely doesn't want to try making repairs three hours from home, or worse yet, to ask Tomas to rescue her. He hates to stop work for anything.

Today she's starting in the southeast, surveying vistas of long-abandoned coal mines – jagged toothmarks gouged into the hills, ridges of hard-packed overburden waiting to be set back into trenches. She sees an ancient dragline, kept as a monument, or simply left for however long it takes steel to biodegrade. In the distance, golden rocks touched with blood-red thrust out of the scarred hills.

She lands well away from the rock formations and lets silence settle around her – or not silence, but wind and whatever sound lies behind or beneath the wind. She gets out and heads into the rocks, feeling the rough surface underfoot, the sudden hard slap of sun. In folds of rock, creeping cedar grows, its small purple berries frosted with fine dust. Must be underground water nearby.

From lifelong habit she picks a few needles and crushes them, inhales the piercing scent, the dust turning moist in her fingers.

She approaches an orange-buff boulder, twice her height, with a neat hole drilled through it by time. Wind sings in the fluted opening, pale sky dotted with cirrus cloud visible through it. The boulder resembles the rock that gave the nearby town its name: Roche Percée. The original Rock Percy, as the locals called it, has long since caved in. The town followed about ten years ago.

Signy looks at the sky, the high, trailing clouds racing across it as if in a time-lapse film. Some people think the sky used to be much brighter, with a depth to the blue you don't see now. Maybe she remembers that.

She leaves a twist of tobacco at the base of the monolith, a practice she learned from Ria, her brother Tomas's ex. They haven't seen each other for a couple of years, but Signy still hears Ria's voice at odd moments: *It's good to respect the spirits. It doesn't matter if you weren't raised to believe that. Just do it.*

Then her own gift: from a leather flask hanging from her belt, she pours water into her cupped hand, lets it dribble onto the stone, staining the rock a darker red for as many seconds as it takes to draw a deep breath and exhale.

She stoops to touch the earth, finding it comfortably hot. She sees ants running up her trousered legs. She slaps them off and moves away from the anthill. Should she consider ants a good sign or a bad? Probably good. Ants are life.

Signy pats the roof of the skyboat as she gets in. The boat might look jury-rigged out of scrap steel, used auto parts, and binder twine, but everything has a purpose and usually works. In whimsical moods, Signy calls her the Valkyrie, Val for short. Val's exterior is painted to resemble white swans' feathers, to invoke the swan cloaks that gave the Valkyries their ability to fly. She has two front seats and a small cargo section aft, holding a rifle, camping gear, and a jug of distilled water.

Signy takes a deep drink of the tasteless stuff, lukewarm in the heat. In a battered notebook on the passenger seat, she puts a tick beside Roche Percée and notes, "Antpile. Creeping cedar. Cirrus cloud."

She takes the boat up to one hundred metres and sets a northwest course back to the old Trans-Canada. At this height, the piloting is pretty basic. The only thing you could run into is a hawk, and she doesn't think any hawk would be that stupid. Besides, she hasn't seen a single one on the whole trip to the rock.

Signy goes through an array of pockets and tool loops in the jumpsuit she made out of army-tent canvas, noting the things she's brought with her: flashlight, trowel, wrench, screwdriver. Flask. Food.

She opens a heavy plastic fold-over bag and takes out what she brought from home to eat, now limp in the heat. Whole grain flatbread, a couple of green onions. A baked potato, sliced, with mustard between the slices. Broccoli sprouts. Spartan but real food grown by herself and Tomas. It tastes fabulous and is gone before she knows it. She wants more, but the rest of the food has to last the whole trip. She has a schedule. Signy can keep to schedules.

After an hour she reaches the old divided highway and changes her heading to west, following the line of crumbling pavement through landscapes of dried grass, long-dead crops, and charred black earth from prairie fires. She sets down briefly near the shell of the town of Wolseley, where once a roadside pump and a printed sign invited people to drink "the best-tasting water in the country." She crouches and scours the ditch for any vestige of plant life. A Saulteaux elder once showed her this spot, where his people gathered herbs. Not a speck of anything alive now, only a few desiccated weeds. Ghost weeds. When she touches them, they crumble to sage-green dust.

Again she leaves tobacco and water. She tries to keep faith, without understanding what it is or means. She doesn't allow herself too much hope.

Back in the air, the boat floats past the empty husks of Indian Head, Qu'Appelle, McLean, and Balgonie, and makes a wide arc around Regina, a city now mainly deserted, and the metal structures that make up the Wrekker colony north of it. She heads west toward Moose Jaw Old Town, where there's a great place for lunch. The concept of going anyplace for lunch now takes a certain mental effort to sustain, but this really is a great place.

Several kilometres from town, the billboards begin, faded and without purpose since no one travels to Moose Jaw by car anymore:

ROMANCING THE PAST: HISTORIC TUNNEL TOURS
TIME TRAVEL TO TEMPLE GARDENS MINERAL SPA
THREE CREEKS SUMMER THEATRE FESTIVAL
LAST CHANCE CASINO CAPERS

Incredibly, the city still functions, at least the core of it does. Decades ago, people believed tourism would solve the city's economic problems, but who could have imagined it would literally keep the city from extinction? Nobody wants to be that right. The deep aquifer feeding the spas drives the city's economy now, and the water is carefully recycled. Glass-enclosed hydroponic farms cover the scars of dead neighbourhoods. The growing season, when there's enough rain to grow anything, is nearly seven months long, except for years when May snowstorms or August frosts strike. "Growing season" is now also a difficult concept to sustain.

The first thing Signy sees of the town is a golf course, its narrow fairways a lovely pale lime, its greens lush emerald. She feels a thrill of horror at the idea that anyone now has enough water that they can pour it on grass just to make it pretty. Although she's visited many times, her eyes can't get enough green. It's like time travel and it keeps her coming back.

She enters the city on Athabasca Street, loses altitude until her wheels brush the road. She glides to a stop, gets out and folds back the wings, and continues into town. They have paved streets in this place and cars to drive. True, most of them are parked – you can get around quite well on foot in Moose Jaw Old Town, and nobody wastes fuel, even here. But they'll all be on the street for the vintage car parade in September. Signy's been trying for years to buy a gorgeous '98 Ford Mustang GT Saleen with remote-controlled cantilevered doors, Swan Wings they're called, but the casino manager who owns it won't sell. Not that she can afford it anyway. Not that she's got anyplace to drive it.

The houses have gardens, with scruffy lawns – there's a limit to everything – and the trees have leaves. Signy's eyes throb at the spectacular blobs of green. As she passes Crescent Park, a giant Zeppelin floats toward a landing pad, blotting out a patch of sun. Canopied electric buses wait to ferry tourists to the spas. Signy drives past and turns left onto Main and down toward the old train station.

Nicky Nguyen's is a tourist place, but it's more than that. Dark and cool, with ceramic-muraled walls depicting layers of soil and blue-glazed underground rivers, it feels like an earthen den.

Sara Kappas brings a glass of cold, clear water and places it before Signy. A slice of real lime floats in the water, its pale juice sacs wonderfully discrete, a small miracle. Signy drinks the water down in one go. It's recycled, but with a few minerals put back for taste. Her throat aches with cold. She sucks the juice out of the lime, sudden sharp joy jolting her brain. Behind the grill, Nicky Nguyen waits.

"I've got shrimp from the last Zeppelin," Sara says. "I've got mushrooms, carrots, and broccoli from our hydroplot. I've got garlic, lemon grass, and sesame oil."

"Yes, please," Signy nods, feeling faint. Sara makes food sound like sex. Better than sex.

"Oh, and you can have an avocado with that. Drizzled with a bit of chili oil." Signy nods again, dazed with longing. These days she's hungry all the time. But she likes feeling alert as a wild animal for her next meal.

Sara slices and Nicky stir-fries. The two women, in their mid-twenties, are half-sisters but look like twins. Everything matches. Straight black hair and olive-brown skin, and roundness expressed in their golden eyes, in their faces, breasts, and hips. Together, they're perfectly adapted to life in this artificial world. They seem contained and self-sufficient, with the air of satisfied cats, although Signy can't figure out if the closeness is sexual and hasn't the nerve to ask. Maybe she just enjoys the idea.

She closes her eyes as the air fills with lemon-grass-and-garlic steam. Then Sara's cool hand brushes hers as she sets down the plate. The coolness runs up Signy's arm. She tears into the food, doesn't care what either of them thinks, almost choking in her eagerness to taste, fill her mouth, feel the textures, swallow. To feel her stomach fill like a round, warm ball, as the cavelike coolness soothes her skin, muscle, and even bone. Her mouth aches to the sweet nutty taste of shrimp. The buttery softness of avocado makes her giddy. She's grateful to be accepted by these fecund-seeming women, with their nurturing and their roundness, even if their conversations never get beyond food. If you care enough, they'll feed you. Things you haven't eaten in five, maybe ten years.

A group of tourists from the noon tunnel tour enters and a gust of dry heat follows them inside. They exclaim at the coolness and the decor, and talk about the tunnels, the stories of bootleg whiskey and Al Capone. Maybe when you have so limited a future the past looks more appealing.

Sara moves to greet the newcomers, the women gaudy in orange and turquoise and hot lime. Their close-fitting outfits, made from shiny synthetic material, have geometric cut-outs strategically placed to bare lots of skin while not quite revealing nipples and pubic hair. They must spend a fortune on sunscreen. Sara leads them to a buffet along the back wall. No one notices Signy. She might as well be invisible.

No use staying now. She's getting claustrophobic, as if the walls are real earth that might cave in around her. Signy goes into the washroom, where turquoise-blue tiles make you feel you're at the bottom of a deep pool. Uses the toilet, washes her face and hands with hot mineral water, the heat soothing in the cool room, lets herself drift. For a second she's afraid to go out again, afraid to face the haze and the white-hot sun.

Over Briercrest, she flies past two of the last grain elevators on the prairies, a Wrekker village of artists of all sorts and disciplines. Painters, potters, jewellers, woodworkers, weavers. Men in one renovated wooden tower, women and kids in the other. Maybe a hundred people in all. They make their living off the tourists in Moose Jaw Old Town. Normally, Signy enjoys seeing places where life in all its variety thrives, but she doesn't stop here anymore even though she finds their work surprisingly good. She can't take their ideas.

They've cobbled together a religion from assorted borrowings mixed with their own strange notions. Drought has come because the sun is angry – no one prays to the sun anymore. They try to set this right on behalf of the entire human race. Their festivals are the solstices and equinoxes, when they can, if they choose, have sex. Otherwise they stay celibate. They have rather splendid dances around bonfires in summer. In winter, if there's enough snow, they build snow houses where people go to fast and purify themselves. If they live pure lives, the rains will come back. *Sunnies,* people call them.

Everyone is watched to make sure there are no slippages in orthodoxy. Continued drought is seen as a sign that some people do not believe as they should. These recalcitrants must be discovered and forced to leave. Discovering them involves elaborate spying and tale-telling that keeps everyone busy.

It's not only the ideas she minds, but the absolute single-mindedness – no, the fanaticism – with which they state them and teach them to their children. It's the expression in their eyes, the absolute knowing that they're right. She doesn't see how a bunch of ordinary prairie folk, many of them raised in the mild and reasonable embrace of the United Church, could have founded this absolutist kingdom in less than a decade after the original inhabitants left.

She keeps the Valkyrie headed southeast and floats over the

badlands around what was once Avonlea, then turns west into the hills beyond the old Claybank brick plant. Over a crumbling stone farmhouse, three storeys with turrets, somebody's crazed imperial dream. Over the remains of fences or the imprint of holes where fence posts used to be. A hawk flies by, missing the boat by a hand's breadth, then dives. It has to be a good sign. A mouse is wildlife. Hawkfood.

But no one takes mice for granted now, not since the hantavirus outbreak in 2011. Deer mice overran the south country like a pale grey river, death in their urine and saliva, which carried a virus that could remain quiescent for weeks or months, lurking in barns or closed-up cottages, waiting for someone to come along and make the mistake of breathing.

She flies the boat up hills, climbing the wide ridges into a sun dimmed by dust, a sun like the inside of a fat blood orange. She tops the highest formation, the last wave of hillside, and floats down to the brittle grass, the landing so soft she can hardly pinpoint the moment of contact. As the boat slows and stops, she gazes over the southwest for what must be more than a hundred kilometres. The red tint in the sky and on the grass makes her think of photographs of Mars. Her own private Mars.

Farther south, in the American plains, it's even worse. In places, there are no people for hundreds of kilometres and the topsoil has long since been lost. When the wind blows, bits of South Dakota and Nebraska and Kansas and Iowa commingle here with the local dust.

2. SIGNY'S CABIN

Built into the side of the hill, Signy's cabin looks smaller than it is. Maybe ten metres across the front, worn and shabby, it has an aura of romantic decrepitude. Makes a person want to get inside its world, take up another life, maybe as a cowboy riding the range.

Signy feels that pull, even knowing that there's no way she could make a living here. But the cabin makes her feel that one day things might change back, and she could be part of that change.

The outside walls have been sanded and softened by wind. The paint is long gone from the silvery shiplap, and only a few chips of flaking white cling to the window trim. The place looks long deserted, like all the others left standing, or partly standing, around here, but is sealed and protected in a dozen ways invisible to the casual eye. Heavy, airtight weatherstripping, triple-paned windows, motion-activated video surveillance, and solar-powered electronic locks Signy invented herself. Signy the engineer – one of her favourite gigs. There isn't a hole or crevice for so much as a grain of dust to get in. Or a deer mouse. An electric fence defends the perimeter, snaking across pale grass that crumbles underfoot as if it had been burned by more than the sun's fire.

Signy punches in codes on a small remote clipped to her belt, hears the click as the locks release.

Inside, everything's still very clean. The solar heating and cooling system keeps the temperature a uniform twenty-four degrees Celsius, blissfully cool on this hot day.

She feels herself being absorbed into her own place: her retreat, her secret den. Not even Tomas or her son David are allowed to come here. Clean oak floors and pine panelling give the larger room, both living room and kitchen, visual warmth. Comfortable old furniture, a sofa, a leather easy chair, an old wooden table and chairs, all suggest an earlier time. The bathroom, a former bedroom, is lined, floor, walls, and ceiling, with deep green tiles, cast with fossil images: nautilus, trilobite, fern, dragonfly. In the bedroom, an iron bedstead wears a hundred-year-old patchwork quilt made from old neckties. Apparently all the women in this area made quilts like these at one time. It must have taken ages to collect enough materials, since neckties were hardly everyday wear.

She hauls in the bag of food and her notebooks and research materials from the boat and stands in her doorway gazing out over the south country. Lines of hills quiet her mind. She closes and locks the door, puts away the food. She drinks water piped in from the nearby spring, for although it no longer flows down the hillside, there's enough for her to use when she visits. She sets dried mushrooms and flakes of red and gold peppers to soak. Makes herself a mug of strong, sweet tea. Pulls a box out of the cupboard and sits down at the table.

The box is full of papers that Signy found when she was retrofitting the cabin, stuffed into a gap between the upper kitchen cupboards and the wall. The papers – and photographs – of Solveig, her great-grandmother, who homesteaded this place in the 1920s and early thirties, before the Depression got too bad and they had to move north. The photographs fascinate Signy. She looks a lot like her great-grandmother, and here in this cabin, she can slip into Solveig's life, imagine herself back in that earlier dry time.

Signy reads through Solveig's account of the small Swedish settlement, as she usually does when she visits. How the good land was gone when they arrived, so they spent a decade trying to grow crops in land better suited for pasture. How the Depression came, and the drought, although they always had water to drink:

> *We have a spring of pure, cold water flowing from the side of the hill, making a patch of bright green against the prairie wool. This water has never failed us. At least, not so far.*

Signy puts the papers back in the box. Shucks her clothes in the bedroom, lies down on the soft old quilt and falls into a deep sleep, her consciousness a globe as big as the sky, a globe filled with lovely deep blue water. Dreams of a woman who could be herself bathing in that water. And then the water falls away and the woman stands on scorched prairie, sun high over her head. She speaks in a harsh, old-woman voice.

"This goddamn sky. Wants to stave in your skull. And the wind, always licking at you, trying to scour you, lick by lick, to bone. I was young when I came to this place. Now I barely remember what that was like. This is where I learned to look over my shoulder. I sowed anger in my heart and ate it for my bread."

Signy struggles to wake up. Solveig has never talked to her in dreams before. Don't think I'm so nice, she might be saying, because I'm not. Signy believes she herself isn't very nice, but thinks a great-grandmother ought to be. In any case, it couldn't be Solveig speaking. It must be her own mind twisting things.

Sleep hasn't refreshed her, it's unsettled her, but there's work to be done, field notes to be made. She steels herself to face the heat.

Outside, Signy squats at the bottom of a cutbank, a slash two metres below the surface. She's created this miniature ravine to trace the root systems of the grass, the complex network of interconnection reminding her of the multifarious pathways of the brain. With the trowel, she picks away a layer of surface soil, maybe a quarter metre square. Already the soil feels cooler against her hand and, she couldn't say moist, but not as dry as she'd expect, although it hasn't rained since May. As she separates grains of earth from the fine, interwoven threads, she's sure, or nearly sure, that the system is dormant, but not dead. Deep inside the earth, it endures only a long sleep.

She sets up her notebook, makes observations, draws one small area of the root system. She trowels up a sample of soil, drops it in a stainless steel cup.

Next she checks a plot about four metres square of similar plants, also bleached in the sun and wind, with the same intricate roots, so tangled together she can't say where one plant ends and another begins. The plants look so dry, she has to resist an urge to get water to sprinkle on them. Instead, she digs one up with her trowel, wraps the roots, the metre or so she can separate out, in a moist hand towel. She seals the specimen in a plastic box, along with more samples of earth. Again she makes drawings and notes.

Satisfied, she goes inside to make her evening meal. Opens a jar of pinto beans and throws in the reconstituted mushrooms and peppers. Adds carrots and fresh thyme from home, and heats everything on a small hotplate. Eats it with flatbread. It tastes achingly, fabulously good, but the one thing she misses is fat – it should have a tablespoon of olive oil in it. Only there isn't any. At least not for people like her. Dragland probably has vats of it.

The outside thermometer reads thirty-two degrees, not cool exactly, but she wants to feel moving air on her face. She opens the inner door and sits by the screen door drinking water and watching the sunset. Dust makes the reds and oranges unusually intense. She tries to identify a scent, grass or sage, anything, but gets only dust. She'd think she was losing her sense of smell, except she could smell just fine when she was eating her supper.

She goes to fill her glass again and hears a scratching against the screen. Fear arcs through her. At the door, what might be a dog, not moving. Why the hell didn't she put the perimeter fence back on?

The thing just stands there. She makes herself approach the door.

A brindled tan-and-grey coyote watches her. A dusty, wolfish tang fills her nostrils. The creature looks so calm, and she thinks of the wolf and coyote lovers she used to know who would have opened the door and tried to touch it. It has that quiet stare in its light-coloured eyes that always unnerves her in dogs. If she avoids returning the gaze, she can pretend to be the farm girl accustomed to animals that everyone expects her to be. But when she looks into a dog's eyes, she always wonders if it's thinking of attacking her. Ripping her throat out. Because it could, and she can never figure out what's stopping it.

So she isn't going to open the door. But it does have a presence to it, and she should be thrilled. A live if mangy coyote. It must be finding enough food to get by: mice or gophers, maybe the odd rabbit. What does the damn thing want? It stands there, watching. That's what she hates, those eyes on her, appraising, accusing almost. But that's ridiculous.

"Go on!" she says, trying to sound tough. "Get out of here! Get away!"

It doesn't move. Might even be laughing at her. And then it does turn and trot away – maybe it waited just long enough to show it didn't have to do anything she said. It fades away down the long slope into the growing dark. After maybe twenty seconds, it merges into the land and she wonders if she imagined it. But its smell lingers. And the feeling of having been judged and found wanting.

Signy punches the remote to restore the electric barrier. She shivers. There's a breeze now. She moves to shut the inner door but stops when she hears the coyote howl, still quite near. The skeins of pure song, like strands of liquid platinum, cut to the heart. She knows she should be glad, in fact part of her is glad, but she turns cold and starts to shake. The way you feel coming out of an icy northern lake on a hot day, chilled to the viscera. As if the coyote had come for her. Or as if he had something to tell her, but she couldn't get it. She thinks she will see him again.

Signy sits in her worn leather chair, hugs her knees to her chest, trying to hold her body still. She has tried to put her memories away in a distant drawer of her mind, but they come back, like this coyote with a dead man's eyes.

Nearly four years ago, in late October when autumn had finally turned the weather cool, she'd come to close the cabin for winter. She'd fallen asleep in the bedroom after supper, curled up under Solveig's old quilt. Most of the ties were satin – grey, slate, amethyst – and she could feel the glossy softness against her arms, even in her dreams. Her feet stuck out from under the quilt, cooled by a breeze from the screen door. Occasional rumbles of distant thunder worked themselves into her dreams. And then there'd been a scratching at the screen and the sound of breathing. She'd thrown off the quilt, made herself go to the door.

What was there had to be called a man, but only because there was no more appropriate name for the animal he was. Shaggy hair, black and matted, shot through with twigs and grass. Skin crusted with dirt, yellow teeth spotted with decay. He smelled worse than any wild animal she'd ever encountered. Maybe like a wild boar, she thought, because she'd never been close to a wild boar.

Incredibly, he wore glasses, held together with wads of tape over other wads of tape, smeared with particles of old food and dust.

In a flash of dry lightning she saw his face clearly. Eyes pale grey, staring. He looked at her with such hunger, a mixture of fear and pleading. Tried to speak but managed only an inarticulate howl, part demand, part whimper. She felt his eyes on her body, and for a crazy moment she felt a response, a kinship.

She'd let him in, given him water and food, not so much out of compassion but because she didn't think she could lock the inner door before he could break the screen door latch. She'd tried to appear calm, but she was nearly fainting with terror.

He'd eaten the food with the absorption of a famished animal, one arm hunched protectively over the plate. Close enough so she could smell his breath, he made snuffling sounds as he chewed. Finally, he stopped and looked at her.

She knew then who he was. Archie Olafsson. She hadn't seen him since high school. His family had abandoned the south country the same time Solveig's did. He'd farmed his parents' land in the colony until they died and then he'd sold up and gone to Alberta – working on oil rigs, she'd heard. So what was he doing here now? Nobody lived in this area anymore.

He regarded her as if she was something else to eat. Either he'd forgotten how to speak, or he hadn't found it useful for a long time. He moved toward her, put out a hand and touched her breast. A sudden smile crossed his face.

"Archie, no," She lurched backwards.

He looked puzzled. Clearly he still knew the name, remembered a time when it had a power for or over him. He moved closer and pulled her against him, the smell of him nauseating. She felt a surge of energy flow through him into her, like a gust of wind flinging jagged glass. He pulled at her shirt, tearing it open.

"Archie, stop!" Strong and firm, as to a dog that misbehaves. Strong and firm, but not angry – anger only makes them mad. "Archie, stop it now! Archie!"

Archie wasn't a dog, and he was strong. As she tried to push him back, his hand swung and he cuffed the side of her head. She felt adrenaline hit, felt the danger she'd been trying to keep out of her mind. She wanted to knee him, but he was too close. Wanted to try all those clever things a weaker person can do to a stronger one. But she couldn't move her arms, he had her too close. And then he did the thing she'd thought must be beyond him: he spoke.

"Signy," he said, his eyes clearing. "You're Signy." She hoped that would be good, that he'd realize what he was doing. Realize he should stop. Knowing each other's names, old associations, that should count for something.

"You owe me," he said, his voice bitter as bile.

"What?" she said, startled.

"This should be my place."

"It was my great-grandparents' farm. You know that."

"I wanted this place," he said, eyes focused now, full of hatred. "I could have made a go of it."

She felt a shift: she was still in danger, but a different kind. She reviewed everything behind her on the kitchen counter. Specimen containers, remote control, long-handled stainless steel flashlight. Archie grabbed one of her breasts, hard, humming low in his throat like a tractor engine on idle, his breath like skunk and ditch and cesspit.

Again she told him to stop, but he put a hand across her mouth as the other reached for her throat.

"It's mine now!" Archie got both hands around her neck, squeezing her windpipe. She squirmed and reached behind her, and snaked her fingers around the flashlight. She swung as hard as she could and then she could breathe again.

The first blow only dazed him, so she struck over and over. She couldn't let him come after her again, not after she'd hit him. He went down and she saw the blur of blood in his hair. Panic like acid flooded her body. She still wanted to hit him, to make sure he couldn't come after her any more, but she had enough self-control not to. She had to get him help, but then what would happen? Would anyone believe her? Would he come after her later? She noticed the time by the kitchen clock: 8:30, and outside it was completely dark. She had to get him out of here.

She forced herself to look at him. His face was a horrible grey, his breathing shallow. She grabbed his wrists and dragged him outside.

She looked up and wanted to dive for cover. Streaming arcs of green and silver cut across an indigo sky. Clouds of pale rose shifted vast distances before she could blink. At times they seemed close enough to touch, flowing through the air with a hum like ancient chanting. She felt she might be the only person alive on this dark plain as tongues of light licked and flicked toward her. They whispered that she was less than unimportant, she was nothing.

Ria once told her that Cree people call the lights the Northern Night Dancers – spirits of ancestors, who may grow lonely and call out to you. If you listen to them too long, they can take you away with them.

She grabbed Archie's feet and pulled him toward the skyboat. She had to get him away from her cabin. Had to use the Valkyrie, even if meant flying into that sky.

Would the Dancers take Archie's spirit?

She managed to get him into the cargo section, blood all over her hands and clothing now. What was she going to do? Take him to the hospital in Moose Jaw? Nothing else she could do. Her body ached from dragging him, but she was still pumped on adrenaline. She could do what had to be done, but she had to calm herself, had to think it through.

She heard coughing. Blood leaked from Archie's nostrils. He coughed again and then there was nothing but her own breathing. Christ! she'd *killed* him. Half an hour ago she'd had a carefully constructed and mostly satisfactory life. Now it was gone, with no way to step back into it.

She tried never to fly at night, because her instruments weren't good enough and it was too hard to judge distance, but she did know the contour of the land. Soon she was airborne and headed toward the glow of Moose Jaw, sixty kilometres away. Flying as close to the ground as she dared, she found the pale white line of the highway south of town. She circled and made a rough landing on the decaying pavement, beside an abandoned gravel pit.

Getting Archie out of the skyboat was the hardest part. He felt different dead, heavier and lumpier. The aurora seemed to touch her face and hands as she dragged him through the shallow ditch and up a rutted trail worn into the grass. Archie's head hit a rock and she half expected him to cry out. "Sorry," she said under her breath. Maybe it was true that Canadians apologized for everything: *I've killed you, but please forgive me for bumping your head.*

Ahead, the old gravel pit cut a deep amphitheatre into the hillside. She dragged and dragged, fighting for balance in the loose gravel, but there was no way she could get Archie all the way to the pit.

She went back to the boat and got the spade from the cargo space. She'd have to dig a shallow hole and cover him with stones. She walked back toward the pit and stopped. Archie was gone. She looked behind her, afraid he would be there, ready to grab her again, but there was nothing, just dark, looming hills waiting to swallow her. She turned in a circle until she faced directly east and then it was easy to see Archie's dark shape on the ground. Two trails came up from the road and she'd picked the wrong one.

When she had a shallow trench dug, she dragged Archie into it and began to shovel the fill back on top of him. Dust soaked into blood, filmed his face and body. Small stones beaded his hair. His glasses had come off somewhere and his eyes seemed to stare at her. She forced herself to close them, warily, as if his hand might shoot out and grab her wrist. When she was done, the mound was more visible than she liked, but who would ever see it?

She fought the urge to roll stones to the grave for a cairn.

Signy had managed to fly the boat back to the cabin, wash up, and stuff the bloodstained clothing in a plastic bag. She cleaned blood from the counter and floor and set the kitchen in order. Dressed in a clean white T-shirt and jeans, she drank hot, sweet tea. Archie inhabited the room as palpably as if he wasn't lying dead in the gravel pit at all. He'd turned her into a person she hadn't met before, someone apparently waiting inside her all along.

There was no staying in the cabin that night. It was just after ten. She could get rid of the clothes and be in Moose Jaw by eleven.

Signy took the boat up again and flew in a circuit of her home territory. East toward Claybank and the old brick plant. South through the Dirt Hills. Northwest over the ancient bed of Old Wives Lake – turned to vast salt flats by drought and the damming of the small river that fed it – gleaming softly, as if the moon had fallen to earth. As the curtains of light shifted and played, the stars seemed also to scatter across the heavens, as if everything was mutable, transient, provisional. But she always knew where she was. On the second circuit, she dumped the bloodstained clothes over the lake bed, saw them flutter toward its pale alkaline face. They would be safe – not even birds went there any more.

She turned on the soft cabin light and the aurora faded. Pulled out a mirror from a small compartment that held her registration papers and scanned her white, pinched face. Rubbed her cheeks and lips to get the circulation going, put on lipstick and brushed her dark blonde hair. Tried to get the wildness out of her eyes. Found a presentable black cotton blazer in her small built-in locker and put that on. She wondered if she looked hysterical. Of course, her brother Tomas claimed she looked that way a lot of the time.

She took a sip of aquavit from a silver flask she kept in the locker. She thought it steadied her, pushed Archie to the edges of her consciousness. She flew to Moose Jaw, floated over Crescent Park, lit up and filled with tourists strolling past the fountains, landed on Athabasca Street, and drove to the nearly empty parking lot of the New Grant Hall Hotel. She dug a small overnight bag from the locker and headed for the entrance. She could pull this off as long as no one touched her, but if they did, they'd surely feel the frenzy beneath her skin.

She walked past a uniformed bellman into a gilded lobby brilliantly lit by chandeliers, dripping crystal like frozen fountains. People milled around her, their faces happy and excited. This place would be busy for hours. A flock of women in orange, yellow, and lime-green satin cowboy shirts and matching Stetsons streamed toward the one-armed bandits visible through the arched entrance to the gambling rooms.

Signy watched a nearby group, fascinated and, in spite of everything, oddly comforted by their apparent normality. For these gamblers were not the young and reckless, but clean-cut folks in their sixties and seventies, more women than men.

People from more habitable parts of North America and beyond, people who'd never come remotely close to killing anyone. Neatly permed women in comfortable clothes, with fanny packs instead of purses – for hands-free gambling, no doubt. Tidy, personable old boys flitting through the clumps of women, knowing their scarcity value in this company. There was a gaiety about them, an almost sexual flutter. Like high school kids going to a dance. Murmuring about which were the good machines and how late the casino would be open.

Signy followed neon-lit footsteps into the slot room, stopped to watch a short, brightly dressed woman in her fifties, her body jerking to the throbbing beat of cowboy rock, jamming tokens into a machine. Her arms, bare in a purple tank top, blossomed with brilliant purple and black tattoos.

"Come on, plums," she murmured, "come on." Suddenly a line of purple fruit formed across the bright screen. A brittle laugh spurted from the woman as her machine emitted a synthesized metallic gurgle that made Signy think of a robot's orgasm.

"Plums!" the woman called to no one and everyone. "Plums! I win!" A few people turned to see what was happening and the woman glanced up at Signy. "Plums play real good," she crooned as the machine spat pewter-coloured tokens like rain.

A woman at a nearby machine, her brass-coloured hair hanging in clumps, her glossy red fingernails so long they curved like a bird's talons, gave the plum woman a hostile glare. The plain white plastic tub the casino issued to customers to hold their stakes was, in her case, nearly empty. She stared at it, chewing at her bright red lipstick with a ferocious emotion Signy couldn't identify.

Signy took a deep breath. This was what she needed, something surreal. She could fit in here all right. Hysterical or not, who was going to notice? She turned and headed for the front desk.

Registration – a piece of cake. Her credit card good, although she had to keep her face from registering panic at the $500 price tag for the simplest room. "Here for the poker tables?" the pleasant young man asked.

"I might give them a try," she said, "but I really came for the hot pools." He gave her a confiding smile, as if he knew she was there for the gambling but didn't like to admit it. Perfect. And to think she'd always been afraid to act in school plays.

"I thought I'd go for a stroll," she said. "Is that all right? I mean, is it safe?"

The young guy, *the kid* as she saw him, smiled. "Sure," he said. "There'll be people on the streets for hours yet. Besides, this is Moose Jaw. The Friendly City."

She gave a small, polite laugh. "So I've heard." She started to walk away, and then turned back. "Oh, is there a liquor store nearby? I've heard you can find some amazing stuff here." She knew the answer, but in case anyone ever asked, she wanted him to remember her.

"Sure thing," he said. "At the bottom of Main Street. In the old railway station."

"Right," she said. "That's easy. Thanks."

Her room was a tasteful mix of antiques and reproduction William Morris fabrics and wallpapers, with soothing sage green- and raspberry-coloured velvet curtains. She wanted to sit at the carved walnut desk and feel like the little Victorian girl the room wanted her to be, but she needed to get some air before midnight.

There were lots of people on the streets, walking between spas and casinos or emerging from a musical play about the days of Al Capone, who was supposed to have holed up in Moose Jaw during Prohibition. Clusters of people wore similar or even identical outfits. She followed a laughing group in straw boaters into the brightly lit station. Only it wasn't a railway station anymore, it was the best liquor store she'd ever visited. The former cathedral to rail travel was now a cathedral to booze, with jewel-coloured wines, whiskeys, and liqueurs, glowing in the soft lights, as its stained glass.

Signy strolled past dioramas of prairie landscapes. They featured several of her favourite places: the Big Muddy badlands, where American outlaws hid in caves; Bald Butte in the Cypress Hills; the Athabasca sand dunes. She paused before the display of the Sand Castles, one of the stops on her rounds. The hog's back formation near the South Saskatchewan, scored by millennia of erosion, soared above the river valley.

She sampled aged single malt whiskeys in a tasting room on the west side. Finally, she bought a small bottle of cloudberry liqueur, only $150, and complimented the cashier on the wide selection of wines that weren't being made any more.

Back at the hotel, she purchased a stake of small metal disks and headed for the slots. In half an hour, she was up $1,263 and had been given free sweet potato chips, deep-fried oysters, and a martini by a tuxedoed waiter working the room. The woman who played plums was losing heavily and stopped to watch Signy, a dull hatred suffusing her face.

When this got tiresome, Signy found her way to the blackjack room where the minimum bet was a hundred bucks. Here the people wore glamorous evening dress, with expensive artificial tans and impeccably styled and coloured hair. Women wore diamond necklaces, or rubies in their ears. At least they looked like diamonds and rubies to Signy. A jazz combo played in a corner of the room, old favourites about love and Lady Luck. An air of boredom seemed to permeate the crowd, but below the surface, you could smell the vulture eagerness. Signy tried a few bets. Within a couple of minutes she was down three hundred bucks. She thought about doubling her bets but stopped herself. Time to cash in.

She returned to the lobby through the Water Wonders of the World Room. Ten-metre-square murals depicted great rivers – Columbia, Nile, Thames, Euphrates, Orinoco – at an idealized time in the past when they were deep and wild.

Clustered around the centre of the room, recirculating scale models of the great waterfalls of Canada – Niagara, Takakkaw, Kakabeka – sparkled in spotlights. She stopped by the model of Nistowiak Falls in northern Saskatchewan, the lighting creating rainbows from any angle you watched. She'd been up there only a month ago. Remarkably, it still looked a lot like the model. The Churchill River, unlike most of the rivers in the murals, was still in business. She stood watching and felt everything catching up to her, the aching muscles and nausea of ebbing adrenaline.

Back in her room, she threw up the free snacks. She brushed her teeth, drank many glasses of water, and had a long, hot shower. Did a hundred pushups and, when her breathing finally slowed, fell into the four-poster, pulled its curtains closed, and cried for a long time.

She remembered Archie when he was young and looked like regular people. Last one left alive in his family. Drifting away like the blowing soil and finally drifting back to the old home place. What was he trying to do, farm? Hanging on, way beyond any idea of success or failure? People like that, you couldn't make them go, you'd have to kill them first. She knew that feeling, didn't she?

A dreary conviction washed over her that said she wasn't a worthwhile person. But after all, what else could she have done? And she'd got away with it. She'd even made enough gambling to cover the room and the liqueur. Luck was with her.

Tonight, remembering, Signy still carries the weight of Archie's death. No one ever asked her about him, and for all she knows, the body was never found. She has never gone back to look. A life should not be taken, and no one should be buried without ceremony. She doesn't know what to do about it, except to keep doing her work.

PART TWO

1. SUNTERRA FARM, NORTHEAST OF SASKATOON

Signy makes a circle over the farm, one solitary square mile in the centre of the old Swedish Colony. This is where grandmother Solveig and her family came after they left the cabin, to a colony that prospered for several decades until in the 1960s it began a slow decline. Fluffy white clouds ride high over three quarters of cultivated land and over Solveig's old home quarter, a stretch of unbroken prairie, long grass blowing in the wind. In the centre of all this, their small farmstead. This is her kingdom – hers and her brother's and her son's. Of all places on the earth, home. Secured on all sides by a two-metre-tall, heavy-duty wire fence anchored by thick steel posts set in concrete.

She feels a strong pull to be on the ground, but makes another circuit. Sees her boy, David, walking through the grass. Twelve years old, small for his age, with shoulder-length black hair and deep blue eyes, although she can't see that much detail. She can see his white shirt, long-sleeved despite the hot day, and jeans. He gives no sign of knowing the plane is there.

He appears to be listening to something, perhaps the sound of the wind. Overhead, a red-tailed hawk rides the updrafts.

Signy buzzes the grass a hundred yards ahead of him and sees him jump. He recognizes the skyboat and waves.

David turns to walk back to the house and again Signy sees the hawk lazily circling. It must be finding mice in the home quarter. She'll make a note in her daily log.

Her radio comes alive. "Are you going to land that thing or just keep making noise?" Tomas must be watching from the house.

"I'm coming in," she says, banking in a wide arc to line up with the old road she uses as a runway. She passes over the farmhouse, also once Solveig's, over the whirling steel turbines that power the farm.

"What the hell!" Tomas's voice cracks, a siren blares in the background. "The home quarter! Signy, go back!" He must see something on one of the monitors. Ten of them, in the farmhouse kitchen, give views of every corner of the farm.

She turns back into the wind and sees the trouble right away. A huge machine has taken out a section of the perimeter fence – a tractor linked to a plough, only there's no cab, it's remote-controlled. And no tires, but revolving treads like the undercarriage of a tank.

Now it's in the home quarter, tearing the virgin grass, ploughing a deep furrow, ten metres wide.

"Dragland!" Signy yells. Nobody else has machines like this. Nobody else thinks this way.

"Jesus!" Tomas shouts. "He's gone too far this time!"

Signy sees the tractor rolling toward David as he walks to the house. "David, turn around!" she screams, but he walks on.

No one could hear her from the plane, and certainly not David, who has been deaf since birth.

David falls to the ground, hands clutching his head as though in pain.

Signy can't think what to do. Try to land between David and the tractor? There isn't time. Crash into it? It might not be enough to stop the thing. The radio is silent, Tomas must be coming. She buzzes the tractor, now maybe twenty metres from David. She wills David to see it, to get up and run. Knows he can't hear the giant machine moving toward him.

She banks the Valkyrie to make another pass and now David turns his head and sees the behemoth coming. He pulls himself to his feet. The machine is ten metres away. He stands and faces it.

She sees David stare up at the monster, as if willing it to stop. He doesn't seem able to move, or doesn't want to. He holds his hands out toward it. Signy doesn't know what she's screaming any more, doesn't know how she keeps the plane circling.

The tractor stops abruptly a couple of metres from David. Its red light goes out. David falls to the ground. The machine appears to regard him through its streamlined headlights. Signy knows it's impossible, but the thing looks puzzled.

She sees Tomas running to David, a .22 rifle in his hand. She lands the boat on a level spot just outside the home quarter's thick grass. She runs to her son.

Tomas is already with him, the .22 flung to the ground, cradling David in his arms. "David! What happened?" David watches his lips, but is too dazed to read them.

Signy kneels in the grass, feeling its warmth, its wiry texture. "David," she says, "are you all right?" David is barely conscious, but she can't help saying it, can't help touching his face, his shoulder. "It's okay," she says, "it's okay now." She sees in his eyes that he's taken in her presence, but isn't ready to speak.

"I think David stopped that thing," she says.

"How could he?"

"I don't know." Signy sees the hawk circling. It's been around a lot lately, now that she thinks about it. Hawks aren't so rare here as in the south, but she realizes she's never seen it catch anything.

Tomas follows her gaze, and she sees him thinking about the hawk in a new way too. He shifts David to Signy's arms and grabs the gun. Takes careful aim, almost straight up, pulls the trigger. The object falls to the ground, but in a way no true hawk would. Signy retrieves it, sees where the bullet tore open its synthetic skin. It is a mechanical contrivance suddenly deprived of power.

Dragland. This is how he watches them, with a clever simulacrum of nature. This is the kind of thing he does. But this trick won't work any more.

David lies on the sofa in the farmhouse kitchen, drinking hot tea. Beside him on a wooden chair, Signy watches his pale, thin face. Tomas sits on another chair beside her. Everything is calm and quiet, the hum of the monitors along one wall and the ticking of an old windup clock the loudest sounds in the room. They've been asking David questions and Signy knows he must be hating the inquisition.

Her eyes wander to the desk, to Tomas's personal monitor, showing a complicated system of interconnected filaments taking up the entire screen – a system of roots, like the ones she examined in the cutbank. The image soothes her, easing the frustration she tries to hide from David. Having to take extra care in forming the words. Having to be right in front of him when she speaks. Having to repeat things. Worst of all, still wanting him to hear – despite everything the doctors have told her – what they hear. If only he knew other people like him. So that once in a while he could feel like the normal one.

David meets her eye. "I don't know how I stopped it," he says in his even voice – a voice without normal human affect, as one of the doctors put it, although strong emotion makes it louder. This voice grates on them, although they try not to let on, and Signy knows he's aware that he doesn't sound like other people. Telepathy would be perfect, but that's one trick none of them, for all their cleverness, can perform.

"Please tell me again," Tomas says. "You were walking through the home quarter. The grass made some kind of music. You felt happy." David nods. "And then the music was gone – "

"Not gone!" David says. "Different. Bad noises." Tomas watches him, trying hard to understand.

"Tomas," Signy says. "Take it easy."

But he's too upset. "So you looked up and saw Dragland's tractor. For God's sake, why didn't you get out of the way?"

"No time," David says. "It was right there. I had to stop it." He sees Tomas take breath to speak but cuts him off. "I don't know how I did it!" He's shouting now, his voice harsh. "I don't know! I don't know!"

"Tomas, just leave it!"

"It's okay," Tomas says. "Let it go. Let it go for now." Disbelief and honest bewilderment struggle for possession of his face.

When Tomas says "for now," David's face turns stony, as if he knows Tomas doesn't believe him and will keep trying, approaching the subject from different angles. Signy thinks it's all fantastic, but if David didn't stop the tractor, then what did? She wonders what they're all going to do about this.

Everything is more dangerous than when they got up this morning.

Dragland has never tried to attack them before, not directly. He wants their land, makes offers for it with nauseating regularity. This time he's gone after the home quarter, the untouched grassland that makes their work possible. Maybe he thought that would be enough to drive them away.

Or maybe he wanted to destroy the quarter for its own sake. Nothing complicated, just jealousy. Dragland doesn't own anything like their home quarter, or even their fields of test plots. His fields, vast, genetically engineered, herbicide-and-pesticide-drenched monocultures, have lost most of their organic content. Years of drought have taken care of whatever potential for crop growth remained.

But why attack David? Dragland has never tried to physically hurt one of them before. Something has made him reckless. If he was remotely directing the tractor, why didn't he turn it away when he saw a twelve-year-old boy in the way?

Signy picks up the satellite phone and jabs numbers. She hears the opening bars of the Norwegian national anthem, Dragland's little joke. Someone picks up.

"You have reached Dragland Enterprises," says a too-smooth voice. As if he doesn't know who's calling; as if these aren't the only two occupied farms for a hundred miles.

"Let me speak to Dragland."

"Mr. Dragland is not free to speak with you." Kuiva, Dragland's technical assistant and general factotum, speaks English with a Scandinavian accent.

"Dragland, I know you're there!" she shouts. "Your goddamn tractor is on my land."

"Mr. Dragland is aware of the territorial deviation of Tractor 7."

"Is *Mister* Dragland aware that he nearly killed my son?"

Kuiva seems momentarily at a loss.

"Is he aware that his Tractor 7 ploughed up some of the last virgin prairie in the world?" There's a shuffling noise and then a new voice on the line, raspy, with a slight quaver.

"I prefer to think that the tractor was bringing the land into production. That's what it does." Dragland allows himself a chuckle. "I don't like to see idle land. Dragland Enterprises doesn't like to see it."

"Do what you want with Dragland Enterprises and its ninety-nine sections, all of them dead or dying." Dragland makes a "tut-tut" sound. "But keep off our land – "

"I've made you an offer for that land."

"Keep off, or we'll have to take action." Signy tries to sound as if she believes there's something she can do.

"A very handsome offer."

"You know damn well we'd never – "

She hears a click. They've turned off the phone.

Signy comes into the kitchen where David sits calmly eating lunch. He goes still, as if gathering himself into the smallest possible space. She scans his face, the look of patience and distance in his eyes. How long has he been like this? Definitely not her little boy any more.

Tomas, who has followed her in, carrying some of her gear, sees the look and smiles.

"Oh, shut up," she says and goes out to finish unloading the skyboat.

Later, she's working at her computer when David walks behind her and into the greenhouse attached to the house. This is where they grow most of their food, adjusting the temperature through the passive solar system that provides part of the heat and cooling for the house. Tomatoes, cucumbers, carrots, mushrooms, and herbs grow luxuriantly and flowers – freesias, roses, purple irises – nestle among them. Signy watches David pick up a long-spouted watering can and water the roses, although it's not necessary – there's a completely automated system for water and nutrients. Leaves and tendrils touch his face and hands as he moves. The sun shines softly through the glass.

His face relaxes and a look of joy and peace steals over it. He would probably tell her he's hearing his music. He says it's different in the greenhouse, not as satisfying as the music of the grass, but still beautiful. She gets the idea of music that is all middle register, with pings and gurgles and trills, as if an immensely complex and comic game were being interpreted as sound.

Signy shakes her head, drawn to the descriptions he's given, drawn as she never has been before when he tried to tell her. Maybe because of one indisputable fact: David collapsed in pain before he saw the giant tractor. Because, he said, his beautiful music had turned to tearing, shrieking noise. She tries to imagine what that might sound like. David has said that the music of the home quarter grass has no melody, doesn't start or stop, in fact has no pauses at all. No recognizable patterns or phrasing, but a pulsing, although not at any regular interval. He's read descriptions of musical instruments, although he can't hear them, and reckons that his music might contain sounds like an organ makes, the deepest notes. And like strings: cello, viola, bass violin; and woodwinds: clarinet, oboe, bassoon. He says there are sudden glancing notes like flashes of sunshine.

Wouldn't it be thrilling to hear such a thing? Joy suffuses David's face at this moment, as he stands by a row of irises, his raised hand holding the watering can.

Tomas comes in from the lab and catches her watching, a knowing look on his face. She doesn't care. She has to understand what's going on with her son. She gets up and pours tea, real tea she bought a decade ago, and they sit at the round oak table.

"I thought we were safe here," she says.

"We haven't been safe for five years," he says. "If we ever were. Think of it as wartime."

"Then we'll make it safe," she says. "I have to protect David."

"I don't know what else to do. Anyway, he seems to have protected himself."

"How could he?" she asks. "How could he stop twenty tonnes of steel?" She watches Tomas's face, wants to know what he believes.

"You know what he says. He heard the grass. Heard music. I must admit, I took it with a grain of salt before. Now, I don't know. Music...from the earth and grass, the insects and microbes all together...what an elegant idea."

"No!" she says. This is what she was thinking herself a moment ago, but when Tomas says it, it makes her angry. "David is deaf. I know he is. I'm his mother."

"Jesus, Signy, that is one of the stupidest things you've ever said. You know that, don't you?"

"Thanks, you sound just like Eddie."

"I don't sound like anybody's flaky ex-husband, least of all yours."

Signy laughs. "No, you'd be more interesting if you did, but you've never known how to do flaky."

"Unlike you, obviously, or none of us would ever have had to know Eddie."

"Eddie had his uses."

"Such as?"

"He was good at sex." She says this to annoy Tomas.

"I don't want to know about your sex life."

"He's David's father."

"From a safe distance."

"Hey, I'm sorry. I don't know why I mentioned my sex life anyway, since I don't have one."

"Don't look at me, baby."

"Relax, Tomas. In some other dimension, you might attract me, but flaky as I am, I still see brothers as off limits."

"Good. More tea?" Tomas tops up her tea and they look at each other and start to laugh.

"Goddamn you, Tomas," Signy says, tears of laughter in her eyes. "You've got me missing Eddie!"

That gets them laughing again. Signy stops abruptly as David enters the room and watches them, puzzled. No way of explaining what's so funny.

"I better call Eddie," Signy says. David reads this and immediately goes to his room.

"Do you have to?" Tomas asks.

"Yeah," Signy says. "Tomorrow."

2. DRAGLAND'S CONTROL ROOM

Dragland runs his hands through his long white hair. He sits in front of a bank of computer screens, showing views of his own and the Nilssons' land.

"This was going to be the day, Kuiva," he says. "Everything was ready. This was going to be the last day of the grass. The beginning of the last day of the Nilssons."

"Yes, sir, everything was planned. It should have worked."

"Why do they keep the grass?"

"I don't know, sir."

"Their stupid, romantic streak. All the Nilssons have it. Home quarter, for God's sake, what do they think they are, pioneers? Hopeless, pathetic romantics."

"I don't know what went wrong, sir." He watches Dragland, as if trying to come to a decision. "But at least the boy is safe." Dragland doesn't seem to hear.

"I watched the hawk fly over their field. I saw through its eyes, my land encircling their pathetic single section. And what did I see on my land? Tilled earth, parched and pummelled with drought. Shards of wheat and barley, shrivelled and dried in shot-blade. Dry land, like crackle-glazed pottery."

"Indeed, Mr. Dragland."

"Why is their wheat growing?"

"Well, clearly we're seeing test plots of a new variety they've developed."

"Test plots. Yes, Kuiva, they've always had scientific pretensions. But I'm a better scientist than either of them. So why is their wheat growing? Nothing, absolutely nothing is growing in these parts."

"Perhaps they have a way of watering it."

"Don't be absurd. Did you see any irrigation equipment? No, the plants are smaller than they should be and very dry, but they haven't stopped growing. Barring a sudden hailstorm – there's a thought – they're going to have a crop. A crop, Kuiva."

"We can try again, Mr. Dragland. When that boy's not around. We can start with the grass and then do the test plots."

"So you're saying the boy stopped the tractor?"

"It did seem that way."

"What was he doing there, that's what I want to know. Why didn't he see the tractor in time and run? It's what anyone would do. You know, for a moment I thought of him only as a boy in danger..."

Kuiva turns his face away from the old man.

"We will try again. Soon the design will be complete. One hundred sections of the Swedish Colony – where my people lived on sufferance."

Kuiva makes small adjustments to the monitors.

"He didn't even try to run. And the fury on his face. He raised his hands, as if they held some force..."

"A malfunction, sir," Kuiva's smooth-shaven face, with its high, rounded cheekbones, shows no emotion. "We'll get to the bottom of it, I'm sure – "

"What's that boy done?" Dragland throws the remote control, cracking one of the acrylic monitors. Kuiva flinches. "I couldn't restart the tractor!"

"I'll send one of the other tractors to tow it home, sir."

"It might as well have been a giant boulder. An erratic left by the last glacier."

"I suppose it could have been the boy – "

"And then that bitch Signy. I saw her look up at the hawk, saw her work it out."

"We've got six more, sir. One of your best designs, I have to say."

"I may be old, Kuiva, but I'm old in cunning, too. Do you hear? They'll find out how dangerous it is to be in my way. I'm not ready to go for a good long time, not till I see them gone. But first I'll know their secrets. How did the boy stop the tractor? Why is their wheat growing?"

"I can't do genetic analysis without specimens."

"Then get some!" Dragland's voice rises.

Kuiva waits a moment. "How will I do that?"

"I'll show you how!" Dragland's eyes glitter. "A child could do it."

The screens are dark. Kuiva comes in, holding another hawk. Up close it's easy to see that it's mechanical, but in the sky it would be harder to spot. It doesn't matter now anyway, as this will be a night flight.

"Give me my spy-eyes," Dragland says and Kuiva hands it over. Dragland opens a flap in the back of its head and checks the solar batteries and radio receiver. He turns off the receiver and closes the flap. He checks the bird's feet, screwing them off and replacing them with pincers. He presses a button for infrared vision.

Kuiva takes the hawk outside and sets it gently on the ground. It looks like a real bird in the darkness – a dead real bird. Back inside, Dragland holds the black box that controls it. In a moment, the bird moves, pulls itself together as if by an effort of will, and gathers its wings about it. Its motor whines softly as it takes off into the night.

A few minutes later, it lands in a small stand of Sunterra wheat. The plants are thirty centimetres tall, but hardy, the kernels well filled out. The hawk's pincers open and close, open and close, until they fasten around one of the plants and tear it from the ground along with a few inches of root and crumbling dirt. Then the bird flies straight home. The process is repeated a second and a third time.

When Kuiva hands a plant to Dragland, the old man becomes terribly excited, as if he might pull it apart to find its secret. He steadies himself and examines it carefully. Doing what prairie people have done with wheat forever, he takes a few kernels, rubs them between his fingers, and chews them.

He appears to enjoy it, as if he has a dormant ancestral memory of being a farmer on the land.

He hands the plant back to Kuiva. "Take it to the lab. Do everything you can to it. I want to know what it is."

"Yes, Mr. Dragland," Kuiva says, "that's what you're paying me for."

Dragland looks off balance, as if he suspects sarcasm. "Damn right it is."

Kuiva gathers the specimens, his face blank, his walk, his bearing, neutral.

"Why do you stay here?" Dragland suddenly asks. "They'd have kept you on at the university in Uppsala."

After a pause, Kuiva answers. "I was an anomaly there. A half-Swedish Saami. Or is it a half-Saami Swede? Either way, no family, no culture. Might as well be here, surrounded by nothing."

Dragland laughs. "Is that really it?"

"I get to do interesting work here."

"And whenever you do leave, you'll have enough money saved to live on for the rest of your life."

"I would, sir, yes."

"We'll see what happens, Kuiva. In the meantime, never think you're surrounded by nothing."

"No offence, Mr. Dragland. That's only how it feels to me." Kuiva walks silently out of the room.

PART THREE

EDDIE

1. MANY NATIONS GRASSLANDS, NORTHWEST OF SASKATOON

Grass as far as the eye can see, a vast undulating circle under molten sun. A hundred or more woolly animals pound the earth. Wood buffalo, some of them a tonne or more of muscle, sinew, bone, and horn, race flat out, chased by screaming men, bareback on pintos and Appaloosas. Screaming men and one screaming woman, her black hair flying in the wind. People behind rock piles or clumps of bush wave red blankets to keep the buffalo headed straight for the jump. The wannabes who can't ride do this job.

A wiry, black-haired man in buckskin chaps, riding a quarter horse mare, streaks ahead of the rest, bison streaming around him. Eddie Johnson catches sight of the woman, Ria Nilsson, near him, and takes a moment more than he should to watch her. Dirt flies, the air heavy with it. The buffalo surge, rough gasps torn from their throats, their dark eyes opaque, shiny, toward the twenty-metre drop to the riverbed.

Eddie's mare, Flora, swerves to miss a cow directly in her path. Eddie tears his eyes away from Ria.

The lead bison sense the danger ahead but it's too late to turn. The front-runners spill over the edge, seem to drop into the earth. Below the jump, near the river, people wait for the slaughter. Tonight everyone will eat roasted buffalo.

Eddie urges his horse onward, as if he's ready to follow the bison over the edge. He's nearly out of time. A bull lunges at Flora, one massive horn tearing a shallow gash in her side. Eddie tries to put space between himself and the bull, but hasn't much room to move.

"Eddie! Look out!" Ria screams. The bull only cares about Eddie now, he's going to deal with this one threat. As he veers, Ria gallops close on her pinto, tears a red blanket from around her waist and flings it over the bull's head. Eddie finds a path through the driving hooves, sees bison pouring over the edge maybe fifteen metres ahead of him.

"Eddie," a man yells, "for Christ's sake!" Devan Stone, a few metres behind, turns. Ria turned as soon as she threw the blanket.

Eddie has waited too long. The cliff above the South Saskatchewan River is only a few metres away. At the last possible second, he turns Flora away from the drop. He reins her in and she slows to a walk as the last beasts charge past him and fall from sight. There is a sudden quiet and then the wannabes begin to chatter excitedly.

Eddie pays a thousand bucks for a hunt like this, even though he works on the crew. Helping move this part of the herd down from their northern grazing range. Filling in every gopher hole on the course. Keeping the wannabes who choose to ride safe. The wannabes pay ten thousand.

"Crazy son of a bitch!" Devan yells, coming up beside him on his Appaloosa stallion, indigo with a fountain of white spots on the belly and rump. "You trying to get us both killed?"

Ria rides up, her long hair tangled, face streaked with dust, hands trembling on the reins.

"Goddamn you, Eddie." Her breath comes in ragged gasps.

"Yeah, I know," Eddie says. "Thanks. I owe you one." He can't keep his eyes off her.

"More than one," she says. "You better see to your horse."

"Yeah, I will. You helping with the slaughter?"

"I always do. And I have to get the skulls from the last hunt."

"Why?" Eddie asks.

"I thought you knew," Devan answers. "The elders say you shouldn't leave them. You should take them back where they came from."

"The grazing range?" Eddie's puzzled.

"Yeah, that's the best we can do."

"But why?"

"If you return the skulls to their proper place," Ria says, "then more buffalo will be born."

Eddie hesitates, as if not sure how to ask. "Do you believe it's true?"

"Well," Ria says, "it doesn't have to be literally true, does it? And we do have more buffalo now than we used to. So yeah, I believe it. I believe it's good to do."

"I guess," Eddie says. "Hey, I could help you."

"That's okay," she says, "I like to do it by myself." She rides ahead, leaving Eddie dejected. Devan watches him with a slight smile.

"You think I'm getting anywhere with her?" Eddie asks.

"Not really."

The wannabes in their fancy shirts and handmade five-thousand-dollar boots mill around on their horses, talking in excited voices, a sheen of joy lighting their faces.

Eddie watches them uneasily. "You don't think I'm a wannabe, do you?"

"Nah," Devan says. "Not like those guys."

"My grandmother was Cree," Eddie says.

"Eddie, it's okay," Devan says. "Did I ever say you were a wannabe?"

They ride along for a few moments, watching dust swirl like a new kind of weather. On the other side of a two-metre fence, animal rights demonstrators wave signs: BUFFALO HUNT BARBARIC and SLAUGHTER = DOLLARS. Ria has stopped to read them.

"Eat vegetables!" a woman in an immaculate pink pantsuit calls out.

"Human supremacist!" cries another.

A big guy in well-pressed khaki shirt and pants shouts lamely, "Meat eater!"

"You think not eating meat makes you better than us?" Devan asks him.

Eddie laughs. "I bet you can't *get* meat anymore where you live." The big guy looks pissed off.

"And *you* think because you're Indians, it's okay to kill animals?" the pink pantsuit woman shouts.

"It's more than okay," Ria says. "This is how our people lived and it's how we're going to live again."

"With *tourists* for hunters?" the big guy sneers.

"It's nothing but a profitable business!" says the woman.

Ria laughs. "Business is only for white people, is it?"

The protesters pick up their signs and drift back to their rented vehicles. Most of them will be staying a few miles away at a hotel-spa complex run by the same people putting on the hunt, part of the Many Nations Reserve that starts north of Prince Albert and runs all the way to Last Mountain Lake. Cree, Dakota, and Saulteaux: a kind of First Nations co-op.

Devan rides off to see how things are going in the river valley. Ria watches the demonstrators leave, as if daring them to start up again. Eddie waits until she's turned back to him.

"Want to come to Iqaluit tomorrow for the Midnight Sun Festival?" he asks her. "The top groups from the entire circumpolar region are gonna be there."

"You're kidding me."

"Great bands. Inuit throat singers."

"Now, that I'd like."

"And there's gonna be a special tasting of the last ten bottles of 2010 Nk'Mip icewine."

"Gosh," Ria says. "Who knew there was any of that left?"

"So you wanna come?" He pulls a satellite phone from his pocket. "I could arrange it in a second."

"Another time, maybe," Ria says.

A red light pulses on the phone. Eddie answers. "Sig, how y'doing?" And then listens for a long time, throwing in the occasional brief exclamation. Finally he says, "Gee, I don't know if I can – " And then, "Okay, okay, I'll try." He puts the phone back in his pocket. He looks lost for words.

"What?" Ria says.

"Dragland attacked David."

"Is he all right?"

"Yeah, he's okay. Dragland sent one of his robot tractors into Sunterra. It nearly ran over David."

"On purpose?"

"They don't know."

"He's really all right?"

"Yeah. Sig says he stopped the thing."

"Stopped the tractor? How?"

"They don't know."

"So you're going?"

Horror spreads over Eddie's face. "I'll miss the Midnight Sun Festival," he groans. "I'll lose my deposit."

"Eddie," Ria says, "you're his dad."

"Yeah," Eddie says, "you're right."

Ria smiles. She gallops away as the demonstrators take off in their vans in a spreading cloud of dust.

The next morning, Devan, Ria, and Eddie sit around a gorgeous rosewood table, satin-slippery against the fingers, in the boardroom of the Many Nations culture and recreation complex. It's run by the Saskatchewan First Nations Consortium, of which Devan is President and Ria Director of Operations. Eddie is Technical Director. First Nations and other visitors can study indigenous languages and crafts, visit a sweat lodge or sleep in a tipi, eat buffalo steak and bannock, drink Labrador tea. They can even play eighteen holes of golf if they don't mind the heat. If they're lucky, they can get the autograph of Devan Stone, international movie star.

It's a long way from what any of them could have imagined twenty years earlier, back in university. Ria was a promising art student and Devan had lead roles in all the drama department productions. They both decided to join a student group Eddie, Tomas, and Signy had set up to study climate change. Back then, they all loved a good time – Eddie and Signy especially. Tomas was the serious one, and Ria liked that. Within two years, Ria and Tomas were married and had a baby daughter, Seena. Eddie and Signy settled down together soon after. Devan built his acting career, working all over the world, but always keeping one eye on home, always making connections.

When Ria and Tomas broke up, Ria helped Devan build the Many Nations movement and set up its diverse enterprises. When Eddie split with Signy, he moved to Many Nations to help Ria and Devan solve their technical challenges.

Now they sit in a boardroom suspended from the ceiling of the resort hotel's main concourse – a soaring tipi thirty metres high, constructed of Plexiglas panels. It's reached by an elevator of the same material, hanging from a rail that rides the inner wall. At the top, a short ramp – also transparent, with a barely visible steel rail on either side – leads to the meeting room, dangling over the centre of the tipi.

The boardroom is also Plexiglas, its structural supports all but invisible. The glass floor gives them a clear view to the lobby below. The table is a perfect circle with a polished stone bowl at its centre. Ria, in blue jeans and a sleeveless beaded tunic, places a braid of sweetgrass in the bowl and lights it. She smudges herself with the smoke, then offers the bowl to Devan and then Eddie.

Below, women perform a Jingle Dress Dance. Like bright leaves in the wind, they skim the wooden floor. Silvery cones on their dresses jingle as they move. Drumming anchors the dancers as the high notes of the singers lift and fly like the dancers' feet.

As the sweetgrass goes out in a drift of smoke, Ria closes the glass door and the room is suddenly quiet, the drums a distant heartbeat, the clear floor a blur of colour.

"We'll keep it short," she says. "We want to get you on your way as soon as possible."

"No hurry," Eddie says, watching her hair gleam like black fire.

"Don't sound so eager," Devan says.

"Look, do you want to come with me?" Eddie asks Ria.

"No way. I'm too busy. Anyway, I doubt Tomas wants me there."

"Sure he does."

"He calls at Christmas and on my birthday. Otherwise, I think he forgets I exist."

"Can't explain that," Eddie says.

"He can probably work better without Ria there. Too much beauty can be distracting," Devan says.

Ria laughs. "When Tomas got working on something, he'd go into a trance – you wouldn't get two sentences out of him in a whole day."

"Sounds familiar," Eddie says.

"Tomas was better when Seena was born, though," Ria says. "I'd see him watching her as if he couldn't figure out how he helped produce such a miracle. By the time she was two, he was teaching her biology. When she was five, she had her own experiments."

"She's one hell of a scientist," Eddie says.

"Yeah," Ria says, pride in her voice, "she's helping with their pet project."

"Oh yeah," Eddie says. "The perfect wheat-grass hybrid. Never give up, do they?"

"Seena says it's going well. They've found a way to encourage growth of the root systems."

"And?" Eddie looks excited.

"I don't know. Something about photosynthesis...making it work better? And a hush-hush project Seena's doing. Tom goes up to see her every month or so."

"Sounds interesting." Eddie watches the dancers whirling below. "Maybe they'll tell me about it."

"If we could get on with the meeting," Devan says in his actor voice. "I've made a short agenda."

Eddie laughs. "Fire away."

"Item one, we need you to take a look at the solar heating-cooling system. As you can tell, it's a bit warm in here."

"Well, it's never going to be like air conditioning," Eddie says. "I told you that when I designed it."

"Still, it's been cooler."

"I'll take a look. What else?"

"The water plant," Ria says. "The solar stills are working,

but the output has decreased. Maybe you can help them figure out why."

"I'll look at the solar stills this afternoon and the cooling system the moment I get back." Eddie looks from Ria to Devan. "You don't mind if I'm away a few days?"

"Of course not," Ria says.

"Are you stalling?" Devan asks. "I could swear you don't want to go."

"Knock it off," Eddie says. "I'm going first thing tomorrow morning." Ria raises her eyebrows, clearly asking, Why not today? "I need to check a few things first. Make sure my vehicle's good for the trip. I mean, it's not like David's in any danger."

Ria doesn't answer.

"Right," Devan says. "Then we might as well get some work done. I've got the plans for the new wilderness camps." He spreads a sheaf of papers on the table.

2. SUNTERRA FARM

"Signy, read the signs, that's all I'm saying."

"I am." Signy dreads these arguments when both of them want to win and no one gives an inch.

"We're surrounded by hatred and death. I'm sick of it."

"He's not scaring me off."

"Of course not. Nobody scares Signy Nilsson."

"Shut up, Tomas."

She watches her brother pull out a stack of documents.

"I've done computer simulations. When Dragland sprays, which is whenever he's got a good, strong wind, he programs his planes so the spray drifts onto our land. We have a band of contamination fifty metres wide along our borders. In parts of the farm, it's worse. Soon we won't be able to do our work here."

"We'll get the law on him, Tomas. Even nowadays, there are police."

"And they'll fine him. A few thousand dollars. Maybe more, since this is organic land. The money's less than nothing to him. I think we've done all we can here."

"No!" She's embarrassed by the uncontrolled emotion in her voice.

"Look around, Sig. Everything's drying up."

"More than a decade of drought will tend to do that."

"No rain all summer, then it all comes in September during harvest. Snowless winters. Frost in July. Winds raking the land for months on end. Remember when people thought climate change simply meant it was going to be warmer all the time? That we'd just be having more summer?"

"The land will come back. The weather will improve."

"If we get a prairie fire..."

"We won't start one and Dragland's place is one big fire-guard now. Nothing to burn."

"What if he sets one?"

For a moment she's stumped. "No," she says, "it would never occur to him. Too low-tech."

"Our well is starting to fail."

"We'll go deeper."

"The aquifer is full of minerals. It's undrinkable."

"I'll set up a solar still."

"We've taken what we need from this place. Checked every significant plant."

"This is so like you, Tomas." She knows she sounds petulant. "You won't know what's significant until it's too late."

"And if we lived somewhere else, we might actually meet new people."

"We don't have time for other people."

He looks annoyed. "I was thinking of David."

"Well, he's *my* son!"

"Oh, for God's sake!" Tomas gets up and paces the room. "Has it ever occurred to you that he needs more than we can give him? If we went away, he could learn to sign."

"Why? I taught him to speak and read lips so he could go anywhere and talk to anyone. Not just other deaf people."

"*Go* anywhere?" Tomas asks. "When does he go anywhere?"

They gaze through the door into the greenhouse. David wanders through it, watering tomatoes.

"Shut up about David. This isn't about him."

"No? Yesterday a man tried to kill *your* son."

"He wouldn't dare try again." Is she sure?

"Why wait to find out? We could get research money, finish our work somewhere else. The university, maybe."

"After they kicked us out?" Signy lets her outrage build.

"After you made it impossible for us to stay, you mean?"

"They were going in the wrong direction," she says. "They were costing us years. We didn't have years!"

"Okay, not the university. A small, independent research station."

"What about this farm, Tomas? What about the land?"

David comes in. He tries to follow their lips.

"We can't save this bit of prairie forever," Tomas says. "Not against Dragland." He hasn't seen David. "We can protect our work better if we leave."

"I won't leave," David says, startling Tomas.

"Sunterra isn't the whole world," Tomas says.

"I won't leave my music."

Signy nods at David. "Nilssons have been here for four generations. I know what I'm supposed to do here."

"I wish you'd be reasonable."

"This land holds onto me. Every rock and plant and grain of dirt." Tomas and David watch her. "I don't make sense anywhere else."

"Five generations," David says.

"Oh yeah," Signy says. "Five."

Signy sits in a meadow in the middle of the aspen bluff a few hundred metres north of the farmhouse. Solveig refused to let her husband Baldur clear the bluff and no one has touched it since. It's Signy's private place, although she suspects David also visits.

Up until five years ago she could tell herself the spindly aspens were still alive. Each year they sent out a sprinkling of pale leaves. Now everything is grey except the sky. She smells dust. Maybe Tomas is right. Maybe she doesn't know when to quit.

No doubt about it, if Dragland wanted to get to her, torching this place would be the way to do it. But she's likely right – that he'd never think of it. He couldn't know what it means to her, could he? Or has he already got another of his giant machines ready to come and tear up the skeletal trees?

If he simply decided to kill the three of them, he'd be the last surviving owner. As set out in the original colony constitution – which Dragland surely knows about, since his parents helped draft it – he would inherit their land. It would work the other way too. If Dragland died first, Signy and Tomas would inherit. This is what they've been expecting to happen for the last decade or so, but Dragland seems determined not to die. He's visited the world's top medical centres, had half his body parts replaced. He's consulted eminent doctors, received the finest advice, the best drugs and nutritional supplements. Surely there will come a day when none of this will answer, but there are no signs that his death will come soon.

A few spruce trees stand out among the aspens, their branches rusty with drought. One, taller than the rest, towers over the other trees. She and Eddie used to meet beneath its shade long ago.

She gets up and ploughs through the dry brush to reach it, runs her fingers along the rough bark. It feels cooler than she expected.

Signy reaches into her pocket for her satellite phone and dials a number. "Eddie," she says when he answers, "I really do need you here... All right, tomorrow, then...Just be here."

Signy enters David's room, both bedroom and classroom. He's supposed to be doing his schoolwork but he must have slipped out for a moment. The room has a loft bed, a desk with a computer in the middle, and on the wall, shelves holding his treasures. He has stuff he found walking through their farm and around the yard: arrowheads, stone hammers, harness buckles, glass bottles, unusual stones. And he has things he took from other colony farms as Dragland bought them up. Before Dragland levelled the buildings, David went in and found what he wanted.

He has door handles, nail pullers, hole punches, screw-drivers, drill bits, chisels, dishes, rolling pins, bobskates, pocket knives, fishing lures, decoys, buttons, thimbles, ladles, bodkins, trivets, and oil lamps. Enough to start an old-fashioned country store. He knows where each piece came from, has everything labelled. Once they tried to make him get rid of some of it, but it wasn't worth the fight.

She has come to call David to help with supper, not to spy, but she sees what he's got on his computer screen.

WHAT I KNOW ABOUT US AND DRAGLAND

1. Sunterra Farm is four quarters of land northeast of Saskatoon in the old Swedish Colony. Three quarters are used to test experimental crops. One is virgin short-grass prairie, including grasses, wildflowers, and herbs.

2. Sunterra belongs to Tomas and Signy Nilsson, great-grandchildren of Baldur and Solveig Nilsson, who moved here in the 1930s.

3. We are surrounded on all sides by Dragland Enterprises. If Dragland gets our land, he will have a perfect square, ten miles in every direction.

4. We are like weeds he wants to pull out.

5. There are no weeds anywhere on Dragland's place. He has killed them with chemicals.

6. We are in his way.

7. *He hates us because we are Nilssons.*

8. Dragland was born in 1899. He has lived in three centuries. I don't see how he could remember the first one. Did the Nilssons do something bad to him a long time ago?

David comes in and finds Signy standing over his computer. She feels ashamed.

"That's good," she says. "Quite well expressed." She has trouble meeting his eyes.

"Why does Dragland hate us?" he asks.

"It's a long story. I'll tell you another time."

"Tell me now."

"It goes back to Great-grandpa Baldur and Great-grandma Solveig. Back to their first homestead down south. He was their neighbour and was always jealous of them."

"Why?" David asks. "You told me the homestead failed. Two of their children died and Solveig nearly went crazy. Why was he jealous of that?"

"It's so complex," Signy begins.

"What did you say?" David asks. If there are too many sibilants, he has trouble making out the words.

"It's complicated."

"If he didn't like us Nilssons, why did he come north too? Why did he follow them?"

"In the 1930s it was dry, almost as dry as now. But things

were better here in the aspen parkland. A lot of people made the move north."

"The north is a big place. Why move right beside us?"

"Okay," she says, "you're right. I'm not telling you. I don't know how to explain jealousy and you're probably too young anyway."

"Don't say I'm too young. I want to know."

"I'm going to get coffee," Signy says and walks away. David follows her to the kitchen.

"Why is Dragland jealous of us?" His face goes red. At the kitchen table, Tomas looks up from his work, startled.

"Why does he hate us?" David stares defiantly at both of them.

"For God's sake, why don't you tell him?" Tomas asks. Signy shrugs.

"It's ancient history," she says. "He wouldn't understand."

"Dragland nearly killed him. Can you explain that?"

Signy pours herself coffee, adds evaporated milk, and puts a sugar cube between her teeth to drink in the old Scandinavian way, a practice Tomas hates because it promotes tooth decay. Who cares? she thinks. I'll do what I want. She sucks the creamy coffee through the sugar.

David's still there, giving her that implacable stare.

"What?" she says. He keeps staring. "Oh, all right, here it is, the part I've been leaving out. It's nothing, really. A long time ago, Dragland was in love with Solveig. Your great-great-grandmother."

"I know who Solveig is!" he shouts. "So they were lovers?"

Signy laughs, hearing her kid say "lovers" in his odd voice.

"I didn't say *lovers,*" she says. "I said *he* was in love with *her.*"

"So?"

"So, she preferred Baldur, your great – "

"I know who Baldur is!" His face turns red again. "Did Baldur and Dragland fight each other?"

"No. I told you, Solveig preferred Baldur. They got married."

"Did Solveig and Dragland have sex?"

"Jesus!" Signy says, then notices Tomas grinning. Of course he's enjoying this. David probably asked just to see if she'd hit the roof.

"Certainly not," she says. "Solveig was a well-brought-up Swedish girl – a Lutheran."

"But – "

"Oh, for God's sake!"

Signy hates losing. Getting upset with David is losing. She slams the door as she walks out into the blistering heat.

Next day Signy and Tomas help David with his new project. In the farmhouse attic, a large room with wooden floors and open rafters, they're building a model of the farm and the land around it, the old Swedish Colony, the way it used to look, complete with its own pond and creek. A railroad track runs through and around it, with an old electric model railroad – a replica 1940s steam train which uses pellets to release smoke that looks like real steam. The train belonged to Tomas and Signy's dad.

It's the one thing they all enjoy doing together these days. An escape to a different world, textured, complete.

The land around Sunterra farm looks different in the model. Small mixed farms, many-coloured crops quilted across small fields of rolling parkland, farmyards with wooden homes and barns. An idyllic world, a fantasy of happy rural life. Tomas is building a one-street village with a general store and gas station, what they called a filling station in the old days. His best effort so far is the elevator: SWEDISH-CANADIAN WHEAT POOL NUMBER ONE, it says on the side.

Signy works on the houses and the aspen bluffs that clump randomly across the landscape. The model should be labelled "Swedish Colony, *circa* 1950." Before things started to change. Or at least before people noticed.

Signy sips strong coffee while David paints the elevator and Tomas goes to the basement to get balsa wood for window trims. Working on the model today is a truce, a break from arguing.

Signy remembers their visits to the city when David was young. She took him to various specialists and slowly lost hope that he would ever hear. How could she take him away from this place? Where would they live? In an apartment – in some barracks, to be more accurate – with no room to set up this model.

David switches the train onto a second track so that it can run through the colony and stop at the station. They have placed model people in it, in their plain farmers' clothing. Tucked inside the passenger car, forever riding across the gentle hills, the clicking rails bringing them home from whatever city adventures took them away. People who knew instinctively that they would never leave this place. That their children and their children's children would never leave.

How could they have believed that? Signy wonders. Only a complete failure of imagination could account for it. After all, they could hardly have kept dividing the farms, a problem they had already faced in the Old Country. Although, by some process of reproductive magic, family size had averaged out at just over two kids per family, as if the reproductive organs of a hundred couples had reached a collective but unconscious decision to keep the numbers down. So maybe it could have worked if they'd all married colonists, and if the world had stood still.

The train goes round and round. David wanders off and explores the stuff piled against the far wall. Trunks, boxes, broken furniture. He pries at the lid of an old trunk.

"Leave it," Signy says, "it's locked." But she's wrong. David pops the catch and lifts the lid.

The trunk is full of old clothes. A plain white satin wedding dress and a filmy veil, both yellowed after decades of darkness. David runs his hands over the dress and Signy realizes he's probably never touched satin before, never felt its peculiar lack of resistance. The veil is net with a border of lace gathered around it. A man's black suit has a small hankie folded into a V sticking out of its pocket. A white shirt and gold cufflinks lie beside it. David turns the cufflinks around in his hands, finally seeing how they fit the holes in the shirt cuffs.

Signy is touched by his curiosity. "This is how shirts used to be made. Dress-up ones, anyway," she explains.

Underneath he finds old snapshots – in albums, translucent envelopes, paper bags – and large studio photographs in loose stacks. Several of the stacked photos, hand-tinted in faded pastels, show a young man and woman dressed in the wedding clothes. The woman resembles Signy, but wears her hair up, long braids wound around her head. She is quite beautiful, with blue eyes and blonde hair. Signy watches David glance at the photographs and then at her, probably trying to puzzle out how they can look so similar and yet so different.

Someone has written on the back, "Baldur and Solveig on their wedding day, 1922." Both Nilssons, cousins, so Solveig never had to change her name. Since Solveig, no Nilsson woman has changed her name.

David hands the photo to Signy, eyes questioning. Baldur is handsome in a squared-off way. Square shoulders, angular face with strong cheekbones, and wiry, wavy, dark blonde hair that thrusts up over his head in an unruly pompadour. As if his hair has a will of its own. He bares teeth to the camera in a grin of simple good nature, with a touch of feral joy. She wonders if David sees this, or if he'd have the words to describe it.

"So what was so great about him?"

"What?" His question catches her off guard.

"Baldur. You said Solveig preferred him. Why?"

"He was considered quite a catch."

"A what?"

"A catch. As in fishing: a big fish, a good catch." He nods. He's never been fishing. "I mean, he was considered handsome, in that Scandinavian way. The story is, all the girls were after him. But he wanted Solveig."

"So she married him because he was a handsome big fish."

"More than that. He was good at everything he tried. A natural athlete. Well set-up, as people said. If he'd chosen to compete, he could've been an Olympic athlete. A sprinter. Oh, and he was good at softball. And arm wrestling. He was the perfect young hero. He was Baldur the Beautiful."

"Who?"

"Remember Baldur, from the story I used to tell you? Son of Odin and Frigga? So beautiful and good that everyone loved him?"

"Not Loki. Loki didn't like him," David says.

"That's right. Loki was jealous. Especially of Baldur."

"Like Dragland." She nods.

"Tell me the story again."

"Listen," Signy says, "could we leave it for now? It's a long story and I need to get back to work soon."

David picks up a waxy see-through envelope and pulls out a picture: Solveig, as a younger girl in a full-skirted yellow dress with a wide sash, her arm around a smiling young man – not the one from the wedding photo, not Baldur. This man is thinner, with dark hair and finer features, as if the bones supporting the cheek and nose have been taken out and whittled down and then put back. It gives him an ascetic look. There's no caption on the back.

"That's Dragland, isn't it?" David says.

Signy looks at the picture and sees that David is right. It is Dragland, with his arm around Solveig's waist.

"She likes him in the picture," David says, as if Signy had denied it.

"She was younger then," Signy says. "Later she didn't like him as much."

"She didn't *prefer* him as much."

"Now you're getting the idea."

Signy hears the rumble of a large vehicle pulling up outside. Then someone cuts the engine. She starts putting the photos back. She has to pry the one of Solveig and Dragland out of David's fingers. He lets go when he sees Tomas coming up the stairs.

"Please come downstairs," Tomas says to David. "There's someone here to see you."

Only two people could conceivably have come to see David, as they all know. He doesn't ask who it is, probably has a pretty good idea. He follows Tomas down the stairs.

I had to call him, Signy thinks. The steam engine whistles and spouts smoke. She flips the switch that stops it, marooning the passengers by the aspen bluff. At least they'll have a nice view.

It's Eddie, of course. Signy watches David from the top of the stairs. He couldn't hear Eddie's hovercar pull up, but he sees the dust now through the kitchen window. She can tell he doesn't consider it good news, but he can't refuse to see his own father. Not that he dislikes Eddie, but he doesn't *like* him either. Eddie opens the door and stands in the doorway, as if he's afraid to approach David. Maybe you have to be around a deaf person a lot to have confidence talking to them. You have to learn to trust the deaf person's lip-reading ability, for one thing.

Eddie sidles into the room and perches on the arm of an upholstered chair in the sitting area of the kitchen, holding his old straw cowboy hat in his hand. He's trying to be casual. Signy resists the urge to giggle. He never has been able to relax in a room full of Nilssons.

David approaches him warily, as if he can't quite believe Eddie is his dad. There certainly isn't much resemblance. Dark hair, that's about it.

"Hi, buddy," Eddie says. "How's it going?" His hair is slicked back with gel, a single curly strand hanging over one eye. It looks affected, a bit pathetic, in fact. He wears tight jeans and a cowboy shirt.

"It's going all right," David says, and Eddie watches the boy's face as if trying to get a hint of his mood from his voice, which is impossible. David wouldn't make it easy for him even if he could.

"Signy thought I should come and see you." David nods. "What's this about hearing the grass?"

"I hear something, that's all."

Tomas is making tea and setting out crispbread. His back looks stiff.

"You think I'm weird, don't you?" David asks.

"Nope." Eddie looks up and sees Signy.

She comes slowly down the stairs. "Why don't we show Eddie the farm?" she suggests.

"Do I have to?" David says. Then he seems to realize it would be better than everybody standing around gawping in the house. He grabs a straw hat from the collection on pegs by the door. Signy hands him a bottle of sunblock.

3. HOME QUARTER

It is better when they're outside. As they walk through the ancient grass of the home quarter, Eddie seems to relax and breathe deeper. Whatever else she could say about him, and there are lots of things, he does love the place. She follows them, enjoying Eddie's walk, the way he looks in jeans.

David points out one of Dragland's spyhawks, circling the yard.

"Must be quite the engineer," Eddie says. "It's very lifelike. What's he do, spend all his time watching this place?"

"He's always doing stuff to us," David says. "When he thinks we're not expecting it."

"What kind of stuff?"

"Sends spray planes too close to our land. Machines that knock down our fences. Tries to find out what Signy and Tomas are working on."

"And what is that exactly?"

David looks at Signy to see if it's okay to talk about it: she shrugs. They walk to the field in the next quarter where he shows Eddie the test plots for Sunterra Gold. Eddie looks impressed. Average rainfall has become purely a historical footnote in this area, but here's a sturdy stand of wheat, stalks dry as grass, but the heads filling out. He whistles appreciatively, does the kernel chewing thing. Watching, Signy feels pride in her belly.

"What's it do, make its own water?" Eddie laughs.

"Interesting guess," she says.

"Wow, this could be worth a lot. So what are you guys doing to fight Dragland? You don't want him getting his hands on this."

"Lots," David says. "We're doing lots."

But of course they haven't come up with anything new since the tractor incursion. "We've got spy-eyes too," David says. "Cameras on all the buildings and along the sides of the farm. And a fence with an alarm system."

"Hey," Eddie says, "maybe you guys could hire me to do extra security for you." He sees Signy's sarcastic glance and realizes what he's said. "I mean, maybe I could help you out."

Shading his eyes from the sun, Eddie happens to glance at the wheat a few rows over. "What the hell?" he says.

They find the place where several plants have been torn from the ground, leaving scattered leaf blades, bits of root.

"Dragland's got himself a sample."

"He must have programmed his skyhawk to get it," Signy says.

"Now he's got it, he won't quit till he breaks the genetic code. Must be worth a fortune."

"He has a fortune already," David says.

"So what is it, then, if it isn't money?"

"Signy told him he'd killed his land."

Eddie looks at the hardy plants. "So if he has your new wheat – "

"Sunterra Gold," Signy says.

"Right, if he has Sunterra Gold, maybe he can bring back his land?"

"Yes," David says. "Signy says he's jealous."

"Why jealous?"

"He wanted to marry Signy's great-grandmother. But she preferred Baldur."

"Oh yeah? That would be a hundred years ago."

"He's got a long memory," Signy says. "So have I."

"Yeah," Eddie says, "I guess." He notices his reddening arms. "Oh, Jeez, I better get back to the house. I didn't put on sunscreen."

Signy and David look at Eddie in wonder. Nobody goes out without sunscreen nowadays.

"Can't help it," he says, "I've always hated the stuff."

4. SUNTERRA FARM

They sit in the kitchen over strong coffee. Signy tries not to look at Eddie too much. One part of her thinks he's a flake, a fake cowboy, a failure in life. A failure, moreover, who could have been a brilliant scientist. Another part likes the way his shirt fits over his chest and shoulders and would like to kiss his lips that always have that slight look of petulance.

"Why don't we give Dragland a surprise? Little taste of his own medicine?" Eddie asks.

"Because we don't operate that way," Tomas says.

"What did you have in mind?" Signy asks.

"Don't know yet, but they don't call me Dirty Eddie for nothing."

"Is that what they call you?" Signy asks.

"Okay, not really. But they might if you let me help you. I mean, this guy isn't going away. The more prepared you are the better."

Eddie has sheets of paper filled with drawings spread over Tomas's desk, and topographical maps and photographs of Dragland's land. "God, this was a good place once," he says. "The best soil in the parklands. Always enough rain when you needed it, sunshine when you needed it. Disasters happened someplace else, not here."

"Yeah," Signy says. "God seemed to be taking a personal hand in the business of sowing and reaping."

"I can't believe what the guy's done to it," Eddie says. "What in hell's the matter with him? Can't he go wreck land somewhere else in the world?"

"He's doing that too," Tomas says.

"What else can you give me? I need to know what he's capable of, what his weaknesses are."

Signy goes to her computer, calls up a file she found on a biographical archive on the Web, and Eddie sits down to read.

> Dragland Enterprises is one of the world's hundred wealthiest companies, with assets estimated at eighty billion EuroCan. Owner and CEO Magnus Dragland is also one of the oldest people in the world, having been born on a farm in Saskatchewan, Canada, in 1899. He gave up farming during the "Dirty Thirties" and moved to Toronto where he earned degrees in engineering, economics, and theology. An ordained Lutheran minister, he left the church when his economic activities began to crowd out his religious duties. A story, perhaps apocryphal, tells of his bishop asking him to decide where his truest interests lay – in the pulpit or in the stock market.

Magnus Dragland's investment successes have now surpassed those of the late speculator and philanthropist George Soros. By the 1950s, he was the world's least known multi-billionaire. By the end of the sixties, the major work of fortune building was complete and Dragland Enterprises settled into a pattern of continuing acquisition of companies, and risk management.

Dragland next occupied himself with forwarding research into the prolonging of human life. He personally funded the first experiments in growing new hearts and other organs from human stem cell tissue. He has been able to rebuild most of his vital organs, but attempts to solve the problem of his brittle bones, the result of a rare genetic condition, have failed. His researchers also discovered therapies and treatments for many types of geriatric dementia.

Magnus Dragland, at 124, while not the oldest person ever known, must certainly be one of the most fit, physically and mentally, to ever reach advanced age. However, to have the strength of a man in his prime and to be unable to use it is a dilemma indeed.

"Wow!" Eddie says, "there's a weakness. A mean old bastard who can't afford to hit you."

"Don't get excited," Signy says. "With his money, he can get mean young bastards to do it for him."

Many of Dragland's greatest projects in medical research may never benefit other people. He became the first and only successful candidate for cloned auto-transplant of the iris, a procedure which cost, including the research budget, three hundred million dollars. Two other attempts ended in failure and blindness.

Another interest of Dragland's old age is his patient rebuilding of Saskatchewan's old Swedish Colony where he spent time as a young man. Despite the northern progress of drought, he has tried to turn this area into a model of modern management.

Eddie scrolls ahead to pictures of Dragland. "He does look well-preserved, doesn't he?"

"Which is not remotely the same as looking young," Signy says. The weight of one hundred and twenty-four years still pulls at the skin, although it's tighter than any old skin has a right to be. The young eyes seem to speak of pain and disillusion – and jealousy and anger and the capacity for cruelty.

Eddie closes the file. "I think you should spy on him. I can give you something better than his mechanical hawks. I can get you in at ground level."

"How?" Signy asks.

"Think small. Think gophers, garter snakes, even beetles."

"Deer mice," Signy suggests.

"Or maybe flies," Eddie says. "Hey, wanna go for a ride in the hovercar?"

"Sure," Signy says, trying not to seem eager. "Let's see what it can do." She grabs a hat, aware of Tomas and David looking away in embarrassment.

In a moment they're out the door, laughing, and Eddie

hands her into the passenger seat with a certain panache. Neither looks back at the house.

The powerful engine, which Eddie made from old aircraft parts, fires up with a roar. A cloud of dust billows around them as the thing raises itself fifteen centimetres off the ground. Eddie could have made it nearly silent, but then it wouldn't have been as much fun to drive. Signy always said Eddie was born in the wrong time. He should have been a teenager in the late 1950s, when the cars had power to burn and big curving fins on the rear fenders.

The car takes off, its noise vibrating in her chest and diaphragm, floating on the shallow cushion of air to the aspen bluff. They follow an overgrown path to the meadow, branches snapping around them, and stop near the tall spruce. Signy has a fleeting thought of David, what he'll imagine they're doing. He knows about the mechanics of sex. The first time he asked her how babies were made he was nine years old. She realized afterwards she'd told him more than he was asking for. She always goes overboard, especially on things she thinks are her duty.

Under the big spruce, in the clear space beneath its branches, Eddie spreads fringed plaid blankets, what Signy's parents used to call "car rugs." They creep into a tent of dappled light, like a green-and-gold yurt. Their clothes come off like birchbark, or snakeskins. Signy tries to remember when she last saw Eddie naked. She feels her breasts against his chest. Science will only get you so far.

Afterwards the sun has changed position in the sky and they move closer to the tree's trunk. She can't believe this has happened, but she must have been missing Eddie without knowing it. She'd told Tomas that Eddie was good at sex, but it's not a question of technique. It's more that he's the only man she's ever known who thinks a woman's sexual parts are beautiful. Not just sexy, which he also thinks, but beautiful. And he tells you. Nobody ever told her that, growing up. Nobody told anybody that, as far as she knows. She must have been really mad at him when they split, to have given that up. She can't stop thinking of how good he felt. How good he looked. The acrid taste behind his ears that reminds her of geraniums.

Signy wonders if Eddie remembers their carved initials on one of these aspens. She wishes she could undo them, not because she regrets that time, but because she wishes she hadn't cut into a tree. She touches the trunk of the spruce and feels a current pass between the tree and her hand. The tree is alive.

That night they all sit up late talking, even David. Eddie's leaving tomorrow to check on his six underground Wrekker colonies in abandoned mines, solar-powered tunnel farms where the growing season is twelve months long. When he finishes there, he'll come back and design the new spy equipment.

David is still as his father talks about the long days and nights in the tunnels, where time almost disappears. Warmth: temperate, constant. Light that matches the sun's: without the harmful radiation. Beautiful dust-free crops: brilliant, deep green, untouched by wind or hail or grasshoppers. Living quarters below ground: warm and bright, with no weather of any kind. The first settlers on the plains lived in sod shacks partly dug into the prairie. Now these twenty-first-century pioneers have crawled right into the earth.

"These guys are all former miners, so they're used to being underground. But they like to go outside at night and look at the stars. So that's what I do when I'm up there. It's peaceful, you know? Like the stars are right there...like they're so close..."

He's got David's attention. He can't know that late at night David goes out to watch the stars too. The first time Signy awakened and missed him she'd panicked: you can't call David, you have to find him. She'd done it by thinking of his favourite places, and found him sitting in the grass, eyes wide open, but so entranced that at first she feared to touch him.

PART FOUR

I. SUNTERRA FARM

Signy sits at the computer, plugging in data from test plots. She is starting to think of hot tea, when she hears a vehicle approaching. Because this happens no more than half a dozen times a year, she can usually identify the vehicle. This one belongs to her cousin Astrid, come all the way from Saskatoon, two hundred klicks over crappy and non-existent roads in an old Jeep with a hybrid electric-methane engine.

Astrid Nilsson is a maternal cousin the same age as Signy, almost forty. Signy's mother was Liv, called Livvy, and Astrid's was Mathilda, called Mattie. Signy and Astrid used to be close, although Signy's always been jealous of her. When David was younger, Astrid lived with them and often cared for him while Signy worked – until Signy drove her out because, although she could never admit this to herself, she thought David loved Astrid more. Too late she realized the dangers of letting another person do all the boring, messy chores for your child. Too late she saw her cousin as an interloper, a stealer of love.

Now Astrid has shown up, which is so like her, not giving you the least warning. Eddie must have told her what happened, and now here she is. Or maybe it was Tomas – he and Astrid get on well. Signy tries to control a wave of jealousy, because David is going to be so happy. She goes to his room to tell him, to give him a moment to prepare, because otherwise even happy surprises are uncomfortable for him.

Astrid hugs David in a way Signy could never manage, pats his face and back, makes comforting sounds. "David, I'm so glad you're safe." Love flows out of her – David is more precious to her than anyone in the world. He's more relaxed with her than he ever is with Signy or Tomas. Watching them together, Signy wonders what kind of mother she is, if she can't share her child's love.

"Good to see you," Signy says, trying to meld into Astrid's enfolding arms. Trying to let the tension ooze out of her body before Astrid senses it. Then Tomas is there, genuinely glad, thank God, to see their cousin. She *is* a lot nicer than me, Signy thinks, but nice isn't everything. Or at least she hopes it isn't.

Astrid looks so much like Signy that they could be twins. But all their choices are different. Looking at Astrid is like looking in the mirror and finding someone almost yourself but different.

Astrid has her blonde hair braided and wound around her head like the old pictures of Great-grandmother Solveig. Her silky-soft dress, made of long curving strips of material fitted together like a vertical quilt, follows the contours of her body to just below the hip, then flutters around her legs in a swirl of colour. Light flashes off the satin pieces interspersed throughout. Salvaged materials: old clothing, curtains, neckties, anything she can rework. Signy doesn't know where she finds it all, but dresses like these, sold on the Net, pay Astrid's rent. When she moves, she's a glowing butterfly.

If only Astrid weren't so much prettier, Signy thinks. If only she didn't radiate warmth like a small sun. But how can she be prettier? She just is.

Tomas is making tea and putting out cups and plates. Signy goes to the cupboard for fruit and flatbread and their precious store of honey. Never let it be said that she begrudged her cousin the best they had, not after all she's suffered. Astrid had uterine cancer in her twenties and had to have a hysterectomy, so she can never have children. Signy can't imagine what it would be like to lose her uterus. True, it's always given her all kinds of trouble, but it's a constant presence, another kind of consciousness.

"Sig," Astrid says, "you look great. I can't believe it's nearly six months since I've seen all of you."

"No," Signy says, "it hardly seems possible."

They go up to the attic to see the model. Astrid has brought along a contribution: a replica of Solveig and Baldur's place, a roomy house with fanlights over the doors and gingerbread trim. She's made it out of painted balsa wood, with real windows in small frames. Astrid loves intricate things.

The house is the best thing in the whole model landscape. David moves Signy's trees and bushes around, trying to fit it in. He's more excited about the model than ever before.

"I didn't know the house used to look like that," Signy says, because she has to say something. "All that fancy trim."

"Oh yes," Astrid says, "I went through Mom's old albums. I guess Solveig designed it herself. Later, she got tired of the trim and took most of it off again."

Signy has to admit it, the house is good. It has a presence, a knowingness, as if it holds a secret about life. Live in me and you will find the happiness you seek. Well, she does live in the house and she hasn't found it.

Of course, everything's changed. She and Tomas have reconfigured most of the rooms, added newer, more efficient windows, dropped the remaining wooden trim as it wore out, and finished the whole with vinyl siding. Only up here in the attic does it feel like a very old house. Only up here does she feel the presence of her ancestors.

Astrid has one more gift, which she places herself: a small wooden bench made to hold two hand-sewn figures which are unmistakably Great-grandmother Solveig and Great-grandfather Baldur. She sets them on the farmhouse's open verandah.

Then David and Astrid run the train around the colony, its whistle blowing as it passes the farms. They make it stop at the station, let off people, and start up again. It makes them happy, as if they're living in the model, riding the train, living in the house.

Tomas has already slipped away and Signy is about to follow when David takes Astrid over to Solveig's trunk and shows her the wedding outfits. She fingers the yellowed satin, the cloud of veil.

"Please," David asks, "put them on. I want to see what she looked like."

Signy would have refused, would have asked why she should bother. But Astrid laughs and tucks the dress under her arm. She goes behind a dusty partition and changes, then comes out from its shadow as Solveig. The dress fits perfectly.

"You look beautiful," David says.

"Yes," Signy says, trying not to sound jealous, "you really do."

Tomas appears at the top of the stairs to call them to eat. "Solveig," he says, "just like in the pictures."

After Astrid changes and goes down, Signy stays in the attic to put things away. The bottom of the trunk is covered with the figured paper once used to line drawers. She notices that the pattern – roses twining around lavender ribbons – is a different pattern than the lining of the sides and lid. It's uneven, concealing something. She picks up a loose corner and it lifts away.

Beneath is aged paper secured by a narrow blue satin ribbon. The writing is Solveig's. Signy undoes the knot and begins to read, but it's not the right time, and after a moment she squares the pages up again and reties the ribbon. Puts the papers back in their hiding place.

2. DRAGLAND'S COMPUTER ROOM

Kuiva hands Dragland a short printed report in a black cover. Dragland reads, eyes darting forward, then circling back. He can't control a tremor in his hands.

"You're sure?" he asks.

"I did all the work twice. I couldn't believe it either." Kuiva looks pleased with himself.

"How are they doing it?"

"It's a hybrid. Probably a strain of Durham bred back to native grasses."

"Oh, for Christ's sake, that idea was exploded decades ago." A flush creeps up Dragland's face.

"And yet it appears they have a perennial, where you'd expect an annual... There would be advantages, obviously. Not having to start from seed every year."

"If such a thing were possible," Dragland says.

"The roots are healthy, luxuriant even. They may have discovered a nutrient that promotes root growth."

"There's no trace of anything now?"

"Nothing I can find. There is another possible variable. It sounds far-fetched – "

"Where would science be if everybody worried about being far-fetched? Just spit it out."

"I wonder if they've found a way to improve the efficiency of photosynthesis."

"How could they? Photosynthesis is photosynthesis." Dragland gets up and paces.

"It's just that, if they could do it...the plants would use less water."

"What?"

"If you can make the process more efficient, more water would be left in the plant."

Dragland looks intrigued. "A genetic change, you mean?"

"Perhaps. Either a mutation or a characteristic they've bred for."

Dragland continues to pace. "It can't simply be genes inserted from another plant species?"

"If so," Kuiva says, "it's from a plant nobody knows about." He considers for a moment. "Of course, they're always talking about their quarter of virgin prairie. What if they've found something there?"

"They claim they don't use GM methods."

"So maybe they're not introducing new genetic material. But they could be using GM techniques – let's say, if they found a promising mutation or a way to encourage the genetic capability of plants with superior performance." Kuiva moves around the room in the opposite direction to Dragland.

"You can speed up breeding using marker genes," Kuiva goes on. "They don't affect the plant, but they allow you to follow the development of the gene you're studying."

Dragland tugs his long hair. "My God, if they've really done this...Can't you analyze the genome?"

"Yes. But that will take a few weeks."

"Get on with it then."

"Absolutely, sir." Kuiva hesitates, as if he's trying to think a question through before he speaks.

"What do you want to say, Kuiva?"

"Well, sir...it would be a lot easier if we had their research notes."

"Yes, but we don't have them, and we don't have a plan to get them. I want to know how they're doing it. The plant has too much protein. It's too green. Too healthy. Too successful. I want plants like that."

"Yes, sir."

"Answers, Kuiva. Bring me answers. Soon."

Kuiva leaves the room and Dragland sits down at the desk in front of the surveillance monitors. He thumbs through the report. "It's brilliant," he says. "If they really have done it. But how could they...how could the Nilssons...?" Before he can think, he makes a fist and pounds it into the report.

A look of fear crosses his face. He pats his hands, arms, and shoulders, expecting breakage. He doesn't find any. He leans forward and rests his forehead on the desk, his arms cradling his head, and weeps. After a while, his breathing slows and he sleeps.

When he wakes again, Dragland looks up at the screens. From the spy-eyes looking into the Nilssons' attic window he sees a woman with golden hair braided and twined around her head, wearing an old-fashioned wedding dress.

"How can this be?" Disbelief and longing twist his face. He taps buttons on an intercom panel.

"Kuiva!" he shouts. "Get in here!" The woman turns and he can no longer see her face.

Kuiva appears in the doorway, a little out of breath.

"Sir?" he asks.

"Look," Dragland says, turning to Kuiva, "look at this woman." But she has moved beyond the spy-eyes' vision.

"Where?" Kuiva asks. "I see the boy."

"No, a woman! In wedding clothes. She was right there."

Kuiva looks skeptical.

"You're a fool!" Dragland shouts. "Get out!"

"Look, sir." On another screen, Eddie's hoverboat barrels up the Nilssons' road in a miasma of dust.

"Who is it?"

"The one called Eddie, sir."

"'Eddie sir?' What in hell are you talking about?"

"You know, Ms. Nilsson's ex-husband."

"Oh, him." Dragland's anger fades. "Go back to your work." Kuiva leaves.

Dragland watches the attic monitor, but now there's no one in the image, only the empty room.

On another monitor, Eddie's hovercraft pulls up at the Nilsson house. Dust boiling around him, he gets out, carrying a large parcel and a rifle. He looks around and catches sight of the spy-eyes on the telephone pole that holds the yardlight.

He takes careful aim and the screen with the view of the Nilssons' attic goes blank.

3. SUNTERRA FARM

They sit around the kitchen table after a supper of buffalo steaks Eddie brought. It's the most meat Signy has eaten in years. Eddie is behaving well, being pleasant to everyone and not flirting with Astrid even though it's his natural default mode. Maybe he knows that would drive Signy crazy.

Everyone looks happy in the candlelight. It's not dark yet, but the candles add a glow. It's a long time since they've had supper with other people. Even David and Eddie seem to be getting along. Maybe there's hope there. David admires people who are good at science.

Signy surprises herself after dessert by bringing out cloudberry liqueur. It's the bottle she bought in Moose Jaw on the night of Archie's death. It's the first time she's been able to consider drinking it. She sees Astrid stare at the bottle and realizes her cousin knows what it is. Astrid is the only person she's ever told, and at this moment she regrets it. But Astrid's look is not accusing. Maybe it's good that she knows.

Tomas pours out the last five glasses of cloudberry liqueur they will likely ever taste. Even David gets a small one.

Astrid takes a drink. "Gorgeous," she says. "I'm never going to forget this."

After the cloudberry's gone and Tomas brings out the aquavit, Eddie pulls a harmonica from his pocket. He asks if Tomas still has his accordion, and before you know it they're playing old Scandinavian favourites like "Stavanger Waltz" and "Life in the Finland Woods." Astrid shows David the beat by tapping his hand and manages to teach him to do a schottische with her. Most amazing, Signy is able to sit back and enjoy it. They all act as if they've been meeting forever to sing and dance and drink cloudberry and aquavit. Signy hopes they didn't give David too much alcohol, but decides not to worry about it. She wonders if Eddie remembers how to play any Beatles songs, the ones they learned from her mom's albums.

"Tell me about Baldur the Beautiful," David says.

"Oh, for heaven's sake," Signy says, "the others aren't interested in that old story."

"I've never heard it," Eddie says. "We Johnsons were never big on Old Country stuff."

"I don't think Solveig was into it either," Astrid says. "But once you marry a person called Baldur, it's more or less forced on you."

"Astrid did her Master's thesis on Norse mythology," Signy tells Eddie. "In Sweden."

"So can Astrid tell it?" David asks. Astrid looks at Signy as if to get permission.

"Oh, go ahead," Signy says. "If you must." Through the window the last light seeps from the sky, and the candlelight seems warmer.

"Since you ask so nicely," Astrid says, "it goes like this." She lets herself go still and focused. When she speaks again, her voice is both more formal and more intense, sending a chill up Signy's spine.

"Now Baldur was the son of Odin and Frigga and best loved of all the gods in Asgard, for his beauty as well as his goodness. Loving him was like loving the best part of oneself."

"Sounds too good to be true," Eddie says, and everyone laughs, except David, who doesn't want the story interrupted.

"One night Baldur awoke, greatly troubled, from a dream of his own death. When Frigga asked, 'What is the matter?' he told her of the dream, and for a time she and Odin could think of nothing else. But Frigga was a god, and gods do not sit on their hands and do nothing."

Eddie shifts in his chair but his eyes stay on Astrid.

"Frigga went through the whole world and spoke to every god, every person, every animal, every plant, every stone. And of each she asked an oath: that they swear never to do Baldur harm. And all willingly gave their oath, for they loved Baldur."

"But why did they love him?" David interrupts.

"I told you," Astrid says. "For his beauty and goodness."

"Can you call a man beautiful?"

"Yes, David, you can. If he's Baldur the Beautiful." She waits for everyone to settle down again.

"So...Frigga was happy. She had taken care of the problem. The end.

"But Odin must have guessed it was all too easy. He rode his horse Sleipnir to the world of the dead and spoke to his sister god, Hel. Before he could even ask, 'Will Baldur die?', he was given an answer, and there was no mistaking its meaning."

David is enthralled. Signy can see the happy anticipation of dread on his face.

Astrid continues. "Her answer was, 'The mead has been brewed for Baldur. The hope of the high gods has gone.'

"From that time, fear gnawed at Odin's heart, but Frigga and the other gods believed Baldur was safe. They devised a game: trying to hit Baldur with various objects – sword, stone, dart, or arrow. They played this game over and over. Each time, the weapon fell harmlessly to the ground."

"They must have been pretty hard up for entertainment," Eddie says, and they laugh.

Astrid continues. "It seemed none could strike Baldur. Only Loki knew any different. The son of a giant and thus below the gods, Loki knew a life of anger, jealousy, deviousness, and strife. He did not love goodness and beauty, but he did love to set things and people at odds.

"Disguised as an old woman, Loki got Frigga talking about her journey through the world, how every living thing had given its oath – except one small, lowly plant, the mistletoe."

A groan escapes David's lips. "Oh-oh," he says, "I think I'm starting to remember this."

"'Oh-oh' is right. Loki went into the forest and cut a twig of mistletoe. He brought it to Asgard, to an old, blind god, Hodel, who sat in the courtyard as the gods played the game of Throwing Things at Baldur."

David can hardly keep still. He covers his eyes, then uncovers them so he can learn what happened.

"Baldur himself must have been heartily sick of it by this time, unless he had a bigger head than even your average god."

Tomas breaks in. "I've always wondered why Baldur put up with it all those years. He must have been a bit of a show-off."

"Well, he was a god," Astrid says. "But more likely he went along with it for the sake of giving others pleasure."

"I'd do the same," Eddie says. Signy snorts. Astrid goes on.

"'Why don't you join the game?' Loki said. Hodel laughed, because he was blind and because he had nothing to throw. Loki handed him the small stick and offered to help him throw it." By now David is squirming in his chair, as if he'd like to walk out but has to hear it all.

"I suppose this was more attention than the old blind god usually got. He probably drew a small but gratifying laugh from the other gods: 'Oh, look, even Hodel's going to give it a go.'

"Did Baldur feel a tremor of fear when he saw Loki position the old man's arm? Did anyone else wonder? Where, for that matter, was Odin when he might have been useful? Of course, he believed Baldur was going to die. So: he wasn't there or he did nothing or he moved too slowly. The stories don't say, so take your pick.

"With Loki's help, Hodel threw the twig at Baldur's chest. It pierced his heart, and instantly the model of beauty, grace, decorum, and goodness fell dead."

David is spellbound with horror.

"The grief of all things, living and not living, cannot be described. Frigga felt as if her own heart was pierced, as if her own blood spilled onto the ground.

"But once again, she wasn't a god for nothing. She demanded that the gods deliver a petition to Hel, asking that Baldur be spared. Her son Hermod, probably used to doing things 'for dear Baldur's sake,' volunteered.

"In the meantime, Baldur's funeral pyre was built on a tall ship. His body was placed upon it and all was set aflame. The ship drifted out to sea.

"When Hel heard the petition, she answered that she would give Baldur back to them on one condition: that it could be shown to her that everything in the world mourned him. Messengers rode far and wide. They asked all of creation to mourn Baldur and the world was awed by the sound of their weeping. But then..."

"Trouble," said David.

"A certain giantess sneered and said, 'Only dry tears will I weep. I had no good from Baldur, nor will I give him any.' Yes, you're right. Loki again. Baldur wasn't coming back."

"And he got away with it?" David asks.

"Not exactly. When the gods found out, Loki was bound in a deep cavern. A serpent was placed above his head so that its venom dripped into his eyes. His wife caught the venom in a cup, but when she had to empty the cup, the poison fell on Loki. His agony, as he struggled against his bonds, shook the earth. Many people thought this caused earthquakes."

"Couldn't she have got a second cup?" David asks. "She

could have slipped the second one in just as the first one filled, and then emptied the first one."

"Maybe if this were a different kind of story," Astrid says. "But this is a myth. And who knows what happened when she had to go to the bathroom? I suppose she gave up that sort of foolishness along with sleep and regular meals."

"So that's it?" Eddie asks. "Evil beats out beauty and goodness?"

"Maybe it beats stupidity," Tomas says. "They should have known niceness wasn't enough."

"They should have known Loki had to be there," Signy agrees. "Or someone like him."

"It's oddly satisfying, though," Tomas says. "Not just that Loki had to be there, but that there was no other way this could end."

"Myths are like that," Astrid says. "But you have to wonder why our people kept choosing the name. This is the story our great-grandfather must have heard, over and over, growing up in Sweden. His family, the nice old ladies and gentlemen of Torsby, all of them would have delighted in telling it."

"What in hell were they thinking?" Signy asks.

"Probably it was their way of saying that he was their favourite – that he'd do well in life," Tomas suggests.

"Maybe there was an unwritten law," Signy says. "Every village had to have a Baldur."

"You'd always be looking for the outsider," Eddie says, "the one who wouldn't weep for you."

"Dragland," says David.

"You know," Astrid says, "living in a small place like this, it must have been a lot like in the story. Everybody knows you, everybody's got your number."

"Must've been a hell of a strain," Eddie says, "having to be good all the time." Signy laughs. Eddie wouldn't have been able to keep it up for long.

"You wouldn't know if you were being good because you wanted to or just to impress people," Tomas says.

"If you were truly good," Signy says, "maybe it wouldn't matter."

"I do sometimes wonder," Astrid says, "if Baldur – our Baldur – *was* all that good."

"Well, we hardly knew him. And Solveig was always shooing us out of his way." Signy remembers that the kids always ate in another room.

"I think you should be able to sue your parents if they give you names like that," Astrid says. She turns to Signy and a look of horror comes over her face.

"Oh yeah," Eddie says, "Signy's named after a famous murderer, isn't she?"

Why did she ever tell him? Her mythical ancestor killed her husband to avenge the murder of her father and brother. She set her house on fire with the husband in it, and her kids by him. Then she walked into the house and burned to death herself. Signy has no idea when she first heard the story, or what it's done to her. The word "murderer" seems to hang in the air.

Astrid tries to change the subject. "They should have called Baldur a nice, simple name. Gunnar or Karl."

"Arvid," Eddie suggests.

"Or Thor," Tomas says. "For that you have to be strong, but you don't have to be good or beautiful."

"In fact," Astrid continues, "you probably don't need beauty *and* goodness. If you have beauty, people take the goodness on faith."

Tomas laughs. "Goodness might be only name deep."

David is falling asleep in his chair. Eddie gets up from the table and stretches. Tomas starts clearing the table.

David opens his eyes. "So was Loki beautiful?"

"I don't know," Astrid says, "none of the stories say."

David drifts off to bed.

"What if the natural consequence of a Baldur is a Loki?" Signy asks.

"There's a question," Astrid says.

The monitor shows a view through a single, circular window, a view of Dragland's huge round room. Darkness lit here and there by pools of light from overhead fixtures. A display case in each pool. This is the view being sent by Eddie's new spyfly. The fly can only see things directly in front of it.

"Wow!" Signy says, "so that's what's inside the bunker." She's watching the screen with Tomas and Eddie.

"What the hell is that place?" Eddie asks.

"I think it's his personal museum," she says.

"My Story, The Life of Magnus Dragland," Tomas says.

The image is surprisingly clear. Eddie has told them how the device works. A fly's eye consists of multiple lenses, which allow it to receive information from many directions, but this one is much simpler, with a single lens which can vary its focal length. This is an automatic function, calibrated within certain parameters of probable usefulness, which can also be adjusted manually by Eddie on a remote control.

Eddie's been monitoring the transmissions for an hour. He called the others in when Dragland entered the museum room.

Dragland stands at one of the cases, a cane leaning against it. He opens the hinged glass top and takes out two objects. Eddie sharpens the focus to reveal a carved, silver-handled tortoiseshell comb and a lock of hair.

They see more light spill into the room. Dragland starts, then thrusts the objects into their case and closes the lid. Turns to the source of light.

Kuiva has entered the room. He approaches and places a box wrapped in white paper on the display case in front of Dragland. He has scissors in his hand. He is about to cut the cord when Dragland reaches out and grabs the scissors. Eddie is furiously making adjustments to help them see more clearly.

Dragland begins to cut the cords, but stops suddenly, his face tight with pain. He cries out, face contorted, hair a blazing corona in the light, like an enraged Moses. He grows still. He places the scissors beside the box and nods at Kuiva.

Kuiva opens the box and takes out small pyramidal boxes. He helps Dragland open them. The two men watch for a long time, but whatever they're expecting doesn't happen. Dragland grabs a box and plucks out its contents, a blob that looks like shredded rubber. He flings it and the box to the floor. He holds out a hand and Kuiva quickly offers his arm. They walk from the room together.

“What on earth was that?” Signy asks.

“No idea,” Tomas says. “Something that came in a box. Something Dragland was looking forward to. Only it was a dud.”

“This is working great!” Eddie says.

“If only we could have seen into the box.”

“Maybe another time we will,” Eddie says. “I’ll make a couple more flies and figure out how to get one inside. Hey, I know – I’ll make one that can drill a hole through glass.”

Signy smiles. A number of things are coming together.

PART FIVE

THE SWANS

1. REGINA WREKKER COLONY NUMBER ONE

From the air, two things stand out: a vast building, like an airplane hangar, and behind it, a plot of improbable green about twenty metres square.

Signy circles the building, flies over a colossal heap of scrap metal that appears to be random. But if you look closely, it resolves into an assortment of smaller angular structures. It helps to have an eye for traditional forms – huts, yurts, tipis – to see that this is a village.

She floats around to the east side of the building to land on what's left of Highway 6. Cracked, bumpy, but a good enough runway. She turns the boat and taxis back down the road. The skyline to the south looks wrong even now, with that hole where the Legislative Building used to stand before they picked it up, stone by stone, and carried it to La Ronge. One of the last great make-work projects, when governments still had the resources to do things like that. It was supposed to be a fresh start. Now at least the Legislature is situated on a real lake. In the north, people used to complain that the government ignored them. They don't any more.

She turns onto the side road leading to the main building. A man waits for her at the entrance. As she approaches, she sees the faded sign: "Interprovincial Steel Company." Beside it, newer and handmade, a sign rests on pillars of junk steel hammered to resemble Greek columns: "Toil and Struggle. Regina Wrekker Colony Number One."

This is a joke, as she's come to understand, from people who don't make a lot of jokes. There is no Number Two.

Beside the sign, people have created a monumental sculpture of a man and a woman holding a sheet of worked steel over their heads, both burden and shelter.

Gord Robin stands in the doorway, his body tense, eyes watchful. He's flanked by two guards carrying ancient rifles: a hard-bitten middle-aged woman with rust-red hair and a blond boy in his mid-teens. Gord is a match for Signy, in a one-piece jumpsuit of old canvas and sporting a worn-out felt hat. The guards watch as she and Gord shake hands and give each other a brief, strong hug. In spite of her recent interest in Eddie, Signy still feels a gravitational pull toward Gord's spare, well-muscled body. Of course most people do have slim bodies now, not necessarily by choice.

The boy's face slips into a new understanding – that there's a bond between Gord and Signy. She flashes a grin and he blushes. The woman guard's face remains closed and harsh, not moving a muscle. She probably sees Signy as an interloper, a possible enemy.

Gord takes her on a tour of the place. Through the greenhouse, full of sprouting seeds – broccoli, bean, and alfalfa, grown for the vitamins – and tomatoes and carrots grown to give people pleasure. Past a rough building housing the colony's solar still (designed by Signy and Eddie over a decade ago) which purifies water from a well connected to the nearly defunct Regina aquifer: just enough water for drinking, watering the greenhouse plants, and occasionally for washing. Past houses dug into the earth, their roofs made of the bodies of long-abandoned cars, two layers of flattened metal with an insulating layer of dirt between.

Children dressed in headscarves and long robes stare as Signy passes. Apparently she's as exotic as an explorer in a nineteenth-century African village. So are the kids, in a way. Wrapped against the deadly sun, they look like desert nomads. No money here for luxuries like sunscreen.

They pass women cooking food at large solar ovens shaped and joined together out of the one abundant resource the Wrekkers had when they started this place, the remains of old vehicles. One or two of the women, dressed identically to the children, smile as Signy passes, but most don't turn from their work.

Past the row of outdoor toilets, they reach the plot behind the main building. Signy inspects the neat rows of plants, takes soil and tissue samples, makes entries in a black notebook. She takes deep breaths to remain calm, to keep her hand steady, because the results are way beyond what she'd hoped for.

Inside the great building, in a central concourse, Signy and Gord sit drinking lukewarm tea. It's marginally cooler inside, thanks to a solar energy system that also gives heat in winter. (The individual huts burn wood scavenged from the ruined parts of the city.) The dimly lit interior is part covered market, part town hall, part village green. One corner features classrooms.

"You're pleased with the results," Gord says.

"Very pleased. The observations here will help us complete our research."

"Well then, what have you brought me?"

"Two fifty-pound bags of flour," Signy says. "We don't have much left."

"Not a lot for our work." Signy sees the change in his face: I trusted you. And now?

"I brought you money."

"Money! What kind of money?"

"The only kind you can spend around here. Tourist dollars."

Gord eyes the gold-coloured coins Signy has placed on the scrap-iron table. "Do I look like a tourist to you?" he asks angrily.

"No. But you can spend them in Moose Jaw Old Town."

"What do I need that a tourist would buy?"

"You can buy sunscreen for your kids' faces. You can buy shampoo. Vitamins. Soap. Oranges. Coffee."

Gord's face is turning an ugly red under his tan. "We need other things more. And how am I supposed to go into a tourist store?"

"I brought you clothes. A suit that belonged to," she hesitates, "someone I knew. A clean, ironed shirt."

"Oh, and how do I get there?"

"Surely you've got one or two vehicles that work?" Signy tries to keep pleading out of her voice. She doesn't want this to end badly.

"We don't like to waste fuel."

"I have something else."

"More seeds?"

"Yes. For next year."

"All right," he says. "It's enough."

He looks at her hungrily now, bargaining over. What usually happens next isn't payment, not on either side. But it's not going to happen today.

"I have to get back," Signy says as she gets up from the table.

He stands as well, mouth tight. "Go then. I'll send a couple of boys to carry the flour." He walks away toward a group of teenage boys.

Signy begins the long walk to the door. She has to offer something more. When she catches up with Gord, she says, "How about you give me a list of stuff you want, and I'll get it for you." He waits a moment, then nods.

She heads home much later than she'd planned. At about five o'clock she's flying north along Highway 6 in a strong wind, when the sun dims too early and the air turns sinister grey behind her. Hills and mountains and rivers of clouds ripple against each other, bearing directly toward her, wide as her horizon. They look soft as feathers, insubstantial as smoke.

Sudden gusts slam into the skyboat and she fights for control. She banks in a wide arc, turning back into the wind, and sets down on a stretch of pavement, dodging cracks and potholes. She just has time to fold back the wings before darkness engulfs her. Avalanche, blizzard, tsunami, all those words pass through her mind as the dust storm rolls over her, grey, then charcoal, then black as night, as if ten thousand ravens crowd upon her. She tries not to panic, keeps telling herself there's enough air in the Valkyrie for her to breathe, that she can wait it out. She wants desperately to see something beyond the darkness, to hear something beyond the wind.

When it ends, she ties a scarf over her nose and mouth and goes outside. The air is still too dusty to breathe comfortably. The skyboat is thickly layered in dust. She tries to brush it off the painted swan wings and feels its horrible gritty texture on her hand. She cleans off the windows, checks the rudder, flaps, elevators, brakes, and ailerons. She takes off where she thinks the road is, fighting for purchase against the dust. She sobs with relief as the boat rises into the murky air, and sets course for home.

2. SUNTERRA FARM

Eddie hands Signy a printout of an on-line newspaper story, with a man's face featured prominently at the top. The caption reads, "Torben Hansen, Marketing Manager, Trans-European Foods AG (Luxembourg) visits University of Saskatchewan biotech projects." Torben Hansen is a golden man, with golden hair and skin – even a glint of gold in his amber eyes. His smile shows strong and perfect teeth, or maybe crowns with that touch of imperfection that makes them look like the real item. Signy scowls – she's always hated men who look too perfect, especially if their smiles look too perfect – and hands the story to Tomas.

"What biotech projects?" he asks. "The bottom dropped out of genetic modification ten years ago."

"They've gone back to more traditional plant breeding, but speeding up the process. Apparently they've got a pretty good new dryland wheat with high tolerance to drought and good protein content."

"Ideas they got from us," Tomas says. "Before they kicked us out."

"They?" Eddie asks.

"Pers Dariwallah and his team. They said our theories were romantic. Eco-religion. Now it sounds like they've adapted some of our techniques."

"Such as?" Eddie asks.

"It's pretty technical stuff," Tomas says. He tosses the paper on the table.

"They're going to beat us to market," Signy says. Tomas gives her an annoyed look.

"Don't get your shit in a knot," Signy says. "Eddie's seen the Sunterra Gold plots. He knows we've got something good."

"I didn't know he'd started advising you," Tomas says. "There's a lot at stake here."

"I know there is."

"Hey, I'm on your side, all right?" Eddie says.

"I'm thinking we should get in there before them," Signy says. "This guy might be our best chance."

"He's not a chance of any kind. We haven't finished testing," Tomas says.

"We've got more than you think. I've just been factoring in the results from the Regina Wrekker Colony."

"You still don't have enough."

"In fact, I've been writing up a report, a prospectus, you might say."

Tomas stares at her. She realizes she's made something of an about-face and that he's probably connecting it to the reappearance of Eddie.

"You don't have the data."

"I have enough. I can extrapolate."

"Cheat."

"Oh, come off it, Tomas. Even Gregor Mendel played around with his numbers. A nineteenth-century monk, for God's sake."

"We don't do stuff like that."

"He did it because he knew he was right. And he didn't want to confuse people with a few anomalous results."

"Anomalous results. Jesus, you take the cake." But Tomas can't help laughing and Eddie joins in.

"Timing is everything," she says.

"Timing meaning the visit of the strong-toothed, sun-tanned Torben Hansen?" Tomas shouldn't try sarcasm with her. He's not good at it.

"Could be."

Tomas waits to see how hard she's going to push this. Eddie sits in a chair sucking on a toothpick, fingers tapping the table, knees jerking soundlessly up and down. Never mind, she doesn't need his support.

"We've been acting as if we had lots of time," Signy says, "because that was the only way to do the work. We had to shut out the world, try not to think about what to do when we were finished. But every year that goes by, people have been starving. People who wouldn't starve if they had Sunterra Gold."

"Come on, Sig," Tomas says, "it's not that simple."

"We have to give it to them."

"What's different this year?"

"There's less water, everywhere. Lower rainfall. Advancing desertification. Loss of species."

"Tell me something new."

"When does it start to be irreversible?"

"What we need is a nice ice age," Eddie says, and the other two glare at him.

Signy hands Tomas an article from a Webnews site that focuses on environmental stories.

DRINKING THE SACRED PEARL

This week, water began to flow through new pipelines from Siberia's Lake Baikal, the world's largest source of fresh water, to major cities in Russia and China. Once 1,600 metres deep and more than 600 kilometres long, Lake Baikal has lost ten percent of its water to evaporation in the last twenty years. Formerly polluted by chemicals from twentieth-century industrial plants along its shores, the water is now acknowledged to be the cleanest on earth.

The battle against export has been fierce, sparking bloody clashes between the Siberian environmental movement, Baikology, and the Russian government. Over the past five years, as the necessary pipelines were built, the land surrounding the lake has been bought up by the water export company, Baikalpur. Increasingly, access for neighbouring communities is being denied, and each year their populations, like the great "Pearl of Siberia" itself, continue to evaporate.

Over the same five years, fifty-three members of Baikology have died or disappeared. The Russian govern-

> ment claims the majority of these people have simply relocated. If so, they've left no forwarding addresses.
>
> Baikology is based in the nearby city of Irkutsk. Ironically, Irkutsk is one of the cities now being supplied with water.
>
> Baikalpur and Russian government hydrologists estimate the lake's water will last a hundred years, given the current level of export. No one knows what the empty trench will look like or what the effects will be on the surrounding landscape as the world's greatest lake slowly runs dry.

"We knew that was coming years ago," Tomas says.

"Maybe, but now it's here. All over the world, things are changing in ways that can't be changed back."

"All right," Tomas says wearily. "I'll give it some thought."

"Okay," Signy says. "We'll talk again."

Eddie springs to his feet. "Go for a ride?" he asks Signy.

"Sure." She tosses him the sunscreen and he puts it in his pocket.

Signy glances at Tomas and realizes he's grinding his teeth. "Tomas," she says, "stop grinding your molars, you'll wear them down."

"You know," Tomas says, "you've always irritated me, but I'd forgotten how much more irritating you are with Eddie around."

Signy considers answering, but she's learned when to let Tomas have the last word. Or the last insult. She watches as he calls up Lake Baikal on his Worldwide Encylopedia. There's a colour picture, with stats on everything from its size to the number of islands it has, and brief notes on its freshwater seals and a salmon-like fish called an omul. And history: it's the oldest lake on earth, not just the biggest. People have always understood its importance, always kept it in their dreams.

"Just think," she says, "it's like driving from Saskatoon to Edmonton and never losing sight of the lake."

"Wasn't there a myth about Baikal?" he asks.

"Yeah," Signy says, "beautiful swan maidens on an island."

"Sounds sexy," Eddie says.

"Don't let me keep you two," Tomas says.

"Right," Signy says, and she and Eddie are out the door.

"So if Hansen checks out, we can talk to him?"

"Let's discuss that after we find out."

It's another day, and this time Tomas isn't refusing outright. Signy wonders if he's starting to cave because she's got Eddie backing her up, or if there's another reason. Maybe Eddie and the Hansen business have simply exposed something they haven't wanted to confront till now. "Live in a bubble and do science till you puke" could sum up their past few years.

They've always believed they could achieve what they set out to do, but they haven't had a clear plan about how to help Sunterra Gold find its way into the world – without either getting hijacked for insane profits or sinking like a stone. It was always a problem to solve down the road. She wonders now what they could have been thinking.

"All right," she says, "I'm on it."

"We're taking nothing on faith. Especially not because the guy's Scandinavian."

"Tomas, for Christ's sake, I'm not stupid."

"And don't think I don't see the glint in Eddie's eye." Signy looks at him nervously. "I don't mean lust," Tomas continues. "I mean dollar signs." He doesn't see Eddie come in.

"Hey, I don't need money," Eddie says. "I've got Pocket Eddie." Tomas looks embarrassed.

"Who's Pocket Eddie?" Signy asks. "And how does he get you money? Oh, sorry, is that just one of those names guys have for their penises?"

Eddie gives her a long-suffering look. "Pocket Eddie isn't a who, he's a what, but I think of him as a friend. He's helped me make child support payments all these years – "

"I always wondered about that," Signy says. "But I wasn't going to ask questions in case you didn't realize you were doing it."

"He lets me pick and choose what jobs I take," Eddie adds.

"How does he do all that?" Tomas asks.

"Pocket Eddie is a miniature computer and data management device. I know that's nothing new, but I added a couple of features." He pauses, enjoying keeping two Nilssons silent at once. "First, it's got an iris scanner. It opens its files only to the owner's eyeprint, so it's got built-in security. You can scroll through a file just by reading – it picks up your eye movements. Second, it's got voice-recognition software. You just ask for a file and there it is."

"I could use something like that," Signy says. "I suppose it's got a satellite phone?"

"Yeah, didn't I mention? These little babies are very popular in Europe."

"So you're telling me you're rich?" Signy and Tomas have a few inventions themselves that bring in royalties, but they're not rich.

"Moderately." They wait. "I've, uh, got several million dollars in a Swiss bank from this...and other inventions."

"I should have guessed," Signy says. "All those extreme sports and ecotours. All those 'last of' parties. Weren't you at Last of the Muskox this spring?"

"Well, I've always liked muskox. Anyway, Pocket Eddie pays the bills."

"Let's see it," Signy and Tomas say at once. Eddie pulls it out of his pocket and hands it to Signy. It's about five centimetres wide and nine centimetres high. When she flips it open, the top half forms a screen.

"Could have made it a lot smaller," Eddie says, "but I had to have room for a screen and so you could see the controls."

"I can see we should have another talk about child support," Signy says. "There's a lot of stuff David may start to need."

"Hey, anything within reason," Eddie says. "Anyway, I'm not in this for the money. Or not only for the money."

"What then?"

"I like everybody-wins situations. And I've been thinking. Devan and Ria could come in on this. The Consortium could give you a land base to demonstrate the product."

Signy and Tomas look at each other, amazed. A deal with Devan and Ria would get Sunterra Gold planted exactly where they need it to be planted. And this idea has occurred to Eddie, of all people.

Eddie thinks they're rejecting the idea. "I know you're afraid of losing control, but give it some thought. You know you can trust them. And you'd still have Hansen for worldwide distribution."

"Your idea could have considerable merit," Tomas says. A smile moves across his face. He and Signy laugh.

"Jeez, Eddie, where have you been hiding this talent?" she asks.

"I've always liked to deal. I just need something to deal with."

"Let's check out Hansen," Tomas says. "Then we can talk about deals."

Checking out Hansen is incredibly tedious. After an hour at the computer, Eddie drifts away and Tomas follows, leaving Signy to work through the complex web of international business partnerships. Hansen's company, Trans-European Foods AG, is owned by Transcontinental Environics, which is owned by World Bio-Enterprises, which is owned by a holding company called Universal Development. It takes her nearly an hour of slogging to find this much.

Each level of the structure is a nearly closed system, as far as information goes. The connections are hard to find. Clearly, knowledge is regarded as power by these organizations. Common search engines pull up potted accounts planted by close-fisted company communications departments. She tries university and government information networks, private think-tanks, and international journalism Web sites and gets a few more dribbles of fact, but she has to dig and dig and dig. Slowly a picture of Universal Development begins to form.

She's amazed at the diversity of its acquisitions, which seem to have been chosen to ensure that disasters in any one economic sector, or even in several sectors, can't wipe it out in a year or even a decade. She's shocked at how many common food brand names Universal Development owns and the amount of once-arable land it holds in expectation of a time when food can once more be grown on it. It owns bodies of water she would have assumed were owned by the countries containing them. Universities and other research establishments. Power utilities. Mines and oil fields. Hospitals and other health care facilities. Tourist developments. Shipping lines. Larger by far than the old transnational giants like Standard Foods, Time-Warner, and Bertelsman, Universal Development is truly protean. Signy's been aware of the name for years, but this is the first time she's looked into it.

She thinks of the people who used to own the arable land, now starving or huddled in Wrekker camps in salvage cities, sleeping in shelters made from whatever scrap metal or wood they can find, eating synthesized food doled out by weary, near-beggared governments, wearing clothing discarded by middle-class people back when everyone's duty was to buy new things. Clearly their operational models were at fault. But Universal Development has the closest thing to programmed immortality of any financial entity she's ever seen. Its chains of interrelated companies make an eerie parody of the tangled roots of Sunterra Gold, and like Sunterra Gold they are growing, against all odds, even in a time of widespread disaster.

As she prints out what's available, Signy thinks of the Wrekker colonies here in Saskatchewan. A big one at Dundurn, near Saskatoon, where the armed forces base used to be. They had a lot of military stuff to salvage, including trucks and oversized tents to cut up for clothing. The one north of Regina, in the shell of the steel plant, where Gord and his people process old car bodies. Fuel is the biggest single challenge. Subsistence is so hard here in winter.

You can have a fairly decent life in the northern camps. Nothing like what the Nilssons have at Sunterra, but decent. The camps Eddie designed in abandoned mines, which were once used to grow herbs or medical marijuana underground, are now homes and farms. Solar energy feeds them, and hydrogen fuel cells developed by Wrekker scientists – people who used to work for large corporations until nobody needed them anymore.

She thinks of the people who live the way they've always lived. Tipis. Log cabins. Fishing, hunting. You can still do that in the north, in the last of the forests. Along the few viable rivers that remain after logging changed the landscape forever.

Now that she's done all the donkey work, Eddie and Tomas magically reappear. "Other than an unfathomable imbalance in power," she tells them, "I can't find any reason not to work with these guys."

"So?" Eddie says. "I can be at that meeting. I can cut Hansen away from the university types quicker than a quarter horse separates a calf from its mother."

"I guess you can talk to him," Tomas says.

"Yeah," Signy says. "You can show him my report."

"Okay," Eddie says. "I'll be careful what I tell him. Just enough to get him interested."

"Maybe I'll come with you," Signy says. "I'd feel better."

Tomas pours them each a glass of aquavit.

"Here's to Sunterra Gold," Eddie says, and they all drink.

"And to the last of the aquavit," Tomas says.

Signy looks at her drink regretfully, wonders if she should save it for another time. Then she shrugs and drinks it down.

3. BESSBOROUGH HOTEL, SASKATOON

Signy's always loved this room. The Terrace Room, high-ceilinged and pleasingly proportioned, has an entire wall of floor-to-ceiling windows opening onto a terrace that overlooks the South Saskatchewan River. The river still runs, at fifteen percent of peak flow. Much narrower than it used to be, now that the Rocky Mountain glaciers are mostly gone. Sandbars-turned-islands choke the shallower sections. Snowpack in the Rockies has been high this year, which she knows can occur even during prairie droughts. For the moment, they have a river.

Sitting by the window in the southwest corner of the room, sunlight streaming in, chandeliers blazing, she can pretend she's back in an earlier time. The river keeps the city alive, although whole neighbourhoods stand empty or burned out. Agriculture is gone, except for pricey greenhouse vegetables, but energy putters along, the city fuelled by the free power it negotiated in return for allowing a nuclear reactor on its northern outskirts. The grand old hotel, the Bessborough, still operates, still maintains fine antique furnishings in its public spaces, gilt trim on intricately detailed ceiling beams and mouldings.

The room is set up with rows of chairs facing a dais at the northeastern end. The centre, about three metres square, is empty, with people sitting on chairs on all sides. Near Signy, news networks have television cameras set up. A sign explains that Pers Dariwallah, head of plant breeding at the university, will make an important announcement today about "a once-in-a-century achievement."

Outside, in front of the hotel, demonstrators rage. Signy had to walk a narrow path lined with riot police to reach the front door, slowed down by the tight-fitting iridescent grey suit and high-heeled shoes borrowed from Astrid for the occasion. It gave her time to read the signs.

ABOMINATIONS BRING GOD'S CURSE

STOP UNNATURAL EXPERIMENTS

CRIMES AGAINST PURITY

The protesters had yelled things at her: "Bitch!" "God's going to get you!" He probably already has, she'd thought. But here in this river-facing room, muffled by the hotel's bulk and its ventilation systems, the demonstration cannot be heard.

The demonstrators come from Racial Purity Wrekker colonies, full of people who claim to understand the causes of drought: mixing races God never intended to be mixed. Today they're here to defend the racial purity of plants.

Pers Dariwallah ascends the dais and begins to speak from notes. It's years since Signy's seen him, but he still looks the perfect scientist. His eyes flash, his expressive hands move as he talks about Hybrid 140, the jewel of his research program. Seven years in development. Drought resistant, high yield – at least for the times – and needing a minimum of fertilizer. Requires pre-emergent spraying with a new pesticide developed at the university, and is then resistant to anything less than a Biblical-strength plague of locusts.

Among the many things Sunterra Gold has over this is that it doesn't require spraying with anything. She wonders if they should mention that to Hansen. He probably wouldn't believe it.

Hybrid 140 is emphatically not, Dariwallah is saying, a Genetically Modified crop – not after the GM wheat disaster of 2009-2012 when they had to burn half a million acres of land three years running to get rid of it. No, it's just a hybrid, achieved through a sped-up version of traditional breeding methods, the kind Gregor Mendel got up to. Of course, Signy thinks, that's bad enough for the Purity Police, who know less than nothing about plant breeding. They wouldn't allow any science if they had their way. But none of them will get near this room.

Dariwallah nods to two assistants. A weedy youth begins closing drapes and a severe young woman in the couture version of a lab coat goes to a dimmer switch at the back of the room. The lights dim and that's when Eddie enters, being ostentatiously quiet, scanning the room. He has a great haircut. He wears an expensive suit and his best hand-sewn cowboy boots. People turn to look at him. Signy grins. The boots suggest Alberta, the suit Europe; the slight swagger has all the prairies in it.

Dariwallah looks up from his notes, annoyed, as Eddie takes his time finding a chair. Now he'll have to work to get the audience back. Not only that, but Eddie has taken Dariwallah's chair – beside Torben Hansen, whose slate blue suit enhances his eye colour and brings out his golden tan. The tan sets him off against the room full of pale stubble-jumpers.

The lights fade to darkness. An image appears in the empty centre of the room, a bright and shimmering holo-projection of Hybrid 140, its leaf blades shiny green, its roots strong and healthy.

"In this tenth successive drought year, Hybrid 140 is yielding just under twenty-five bushels per hectare – or shall we say ten bushels to the acre, the way we've always talked in Saskatchewan." Dariwallah chuckles. His voice grows in power as the holo-image rotates in the darkness to allow everyone to see all sides. "Most remarkable, however, is its quality. Protein, ladies and gentlemen, protein the world needs, at twenty percent."

A new hologram appears. Children in a rainbow array of skin and clothing colours run their hands through a basin of golden wheat. A new hologram appears with the same children eating slices of buttered whole grain bread, laughing with pleasure.

The audience, most of whom are from the university and must have been in on the secret, gives a collective sigh anyway. Signy has to admit, Dariwallah knows how to put on a show.

She sees Eddie speak to Torben Hansen, who stares at the glowing projection. Sees him start and turn to Eddie. "That's good, but I've got something a lot better," she imagines Eddie saying.

Eddie reaches into his pocket and takes out his business card and gives it to Hansen. Hansen regards Eddie with puzzled distaste, but takes the card before he turns his attention back to Dariwallah.

"Hybrid 140 is more than just a new wheat." Dariwallah speaks with an intensity close to awe. "It is unprecedented mastery over the vagaries of nature. It is health and beauty and hope for the world's hungry."

Signy brings her hands together lightly as the audience breaks into enthusiastic applause. The lights come up on smiling, relaxed faces. The hologram fades. Dariwallah strides back to what was his seat and offers his hand to Hansen, who rises and shakes it heartily. But he looks disappointed, off balance, as the audience begins to mill and chat. Good, Signy thinks. Something has gone wrong, but he doesn't understand what.

As Eddie turns to leave the room, Signy notices a man watching him, a man with high, rounded cheekbones in a smoothly sculpted face. He waits a moment and follows Eddie out.

Signy follows the two of them into the wide corridor. He's close on Eddie's heels as Eddie stops to ring for the elevator. Signy touches the man's sleeve and he whirls to face her, confusion and embarrassment on his face.

"Oh, excuse me," she says, "I thought you were someone else."

The elevator pings and the door opens. Eddie steps in. The man turns as if to follow Eddie onto the elevator.

"You're Magnus Dragland's man," she says, and he turns to her again as the elevator doors open and Eddie enters. "From the University of Uppsala."

"How do you know that?" he asks.

"I have friends there," she says. "People who knew you." Astrid did graduate work at his old university. "You're a Laplander, aren't you?" She uses the wrong word deliberately to provoke a reaction.

"My mother was a Saami," he says angrily as the elevator doors close again.

"No need to get upset," she says, "Saami's cool with me. So did you get what you came for?"

He stares at her. Talking to nobody but Dragland all the time, he probably doesn't know how to talk to anybody else.

"Kuiva, isn't it? Is that what the old man calls you?"

Kuiva turns and walks back toward the Terrace Room. Signy rings for the elevator.

Signy arrives at the eighth floor as Eddie is knocking on a door. He waits for her to catch up. Devan opens the door and welcomes them into the SFNC's Saskatoon office, a suite that might have looked the same in the early 1900s, tables and chairs in polished dark wood, chair seats and sofas upholstered in burgundy brocade. There are so many antiques in this hotel and in tourist locations around the province. Maybe the hotel owners have found a way to clone them.

"Signy." Devan gives her a hug. "Wonderful to see you. Great suit."

"Astrid's. She's the one with all the taste."

Devan and Eddie do a complicated thing with their hands,

twining and intertwining fingers in their comic take on a secret handshake. Ria comes over and hugs Signy.

"It's good to see you," she says. "How's David?"

"He's fine. He says to say hello. And Tomas says hi."

"He remembers me," Ria says.

"Oh yes," Signy says, "probably better than when you were together." They laugh. Ria is beautiful, her hair streaming down her shoulders in a black waterfall, wearing a plain black suit with blue-and-green quillwork down the lapels and sleeves.

"Looking great, Ria," Eddie says. "How's business?" Signy feels a flash of certainty that Eddie's been flirting with Ria. Harder to tell if Ria's been flirting back. She decides it doesn't matter. She's not going to be jealous of Tomas's ex, it would be too weird.

"My power-and-influence outfit," Ria says.

Devan lights sweetgrass in a ceramic bowl. This office is the only place in the hotel where you're allowed to light anything besides a birthday candle, Ria explains. The four of them sit quietly, hands wafting the smoke around their faces and bodies. Signy feels her breathing become deeper and slower as she contemplates the things it's possible for them to achieve, if they play everything right. The sweetgrass goes out and Ria moves it to a sideboard.

"Nice place," Signy says.

"If you want your business to get respect," Devan says, "you need the right look."

"Don't I know it," Eddie says, striking a pose in the fancy suit, and they all laugh.

Devan pours them each a cup of tea from a silver service on a sideboard, steam mingling with the smoke.

Eddie pulls out Pocket Eddie, opens a file and hands it to Devan, who reads it, then passes it to Ria, who also quickly reads the file. "Wow," she says. "Think what we could do with this in the southern part of the province. Maybe even the American plains states some day."

"That was the plan," Signy says. "But we want to start here."

"Great," Devan says. "What do we need with the guy downstairs?"

"We're thinking bigger than here," Signy says.

"Three-way deal," Eddie says. "You guys, Tom and Signy, and the guy downstairs."

"Why do we need him?" Ria asks.

"Several reasons," Eddie says. "One, he's big enough to keep Dragland off our backs. Two, he's got markets all over the world, and three, he's got the information machine to get our message out."

"But?" Devan asks.

"But unless we sell to him, he's going to buy from Pers Dariwallah. The above advantages will be squandered on Hybrid 140 and when we come into the market, no one's gonna listen."

"So what?" Devan asks. "We could start in the west. Let the results speak for themselves. Reverse desertification."

"We could do that," Signy says. They all think about it. They could create a massive demonstration project, but it would take years to show results. In the meantime, the university's wheat might take over in the rest of the world. Sunterra Gold could remain a regional crop.

"Eddie's right," Ria says. "We should go after the whole package."

Devan looks unconvinced. "Sure? We could be in over our heads."

"I'm sure."

Signy hesitates only a moment. "I'm sure too," she says.

"Okay then," Eddie says, "I'm going back down there and I'm gonna show him what you just saw. Then we'll all meet with him."

"Here?" Ria asks.

"I thought maybe at the resort," Eddie says. "We need to create an experience for him. Buffalo stew and bannock. Maybe a sweat. Meet in the boardroom. He'll love the see-through floor."

"Okay," Devan says. "Pick your time. We'll be there."

"You coming, Sig?" Eddie asks.

"No, Eddie, you do it. You're on a roll. God knows how he'd take to me."

"Hey, I'm sure he loves you fair Nordic types."

"I'll come to the meeting at the resort."

"Okay," Eddie says. "I guess this is the moment."

"Off you go," Signy says. She catches Ria's eye and they break into laughter. Signy hopes to hell they know what they're doing.

4. SFNC BOARDROOM

Sitting in the boardroom, Signy and Eddie watch as Ria and Devan bring Torben Hansen up in the transparent elevator. Hansen gazes down at the lobby where hoop dancers leap and spin, forming patterns of intersecting circles. The singing and drumming feel timeless, as though people have always danced in this place, always will dance.

Hansen touches Ria's arm and she stops the elevator.

With a single strong drumbeat, the dance ends and the onlookers applaud. A group of men in traditional costume begins a Grass Dance. The drumbeat picks up, the singing grows more intense. Hansen watches, entranced.

Eddie's telling Signy about the men's sweat. "I was totally relaxed," he says. "I felt like my mind could stretch to hold the entire universe, or pull in to focus on a grain of dust."

"What about Hansen?"

"He loved it. Spent the whole time in a full lotus with his eyes closed and this look of ecstasy plastered on his face. Danish Buddha look. Sweat on his skin so fine you could barely see it."

"He's going to dine out on this for months." Signy mimics Hansen's accent: "'Went to a real Native sweat lodge. In *Sas*-ka-chew-*an*. Extraordinary thing. Everyone should do it at least once.' He'll rank it with his Kenyan photo-safari, when he drank cow's blood with the Masai." They laugh. Hansen had talked about the cow's blood during last night's dinner.

"Sig, I had a lot of time to think in the sweat," Eddie says.

"I suppose that's the idea."

"There's nowhere to go but inside. I could see all my crummy habits – "

"Which ones? Love of cheap thrills? Failure as a father?"

"I thought about David and this music he hears. And I thought, why not? I mean, there's mutations all the time in nature. All along we thought he was missing something. Nobody ever thought he might have something extra."

Eddie's face looks young and smooth. It reminds her of the way he looked when they were first lovers.

"Eddie," she asks, "did you have something going with Astrid?"

He looks ashamed. "Yeah, after you and I broke up."

"God, how could you?"

"I think I wanted to get back at you."

"But I never even knew."

"I'm sorry."

"Oh, Eddie," she says. They both have tears in their eyes.

The elevator is moving again. It reaches the level of the boardroom. Devan leads Hansen to the ramp that leads over open space to the chamber. Hansen stops in his tracks. Maybe he's never seen a transparent ramp before, the steel supports and safety rail so cleverly hidden. Devan steps forward, suspended over the glowing canyon. Hansen makes himself step onto the ramp. His hand grips the rail.

This was a good idea, Signy thinks. Let the guy find out what's going on in this place. Let him have an experience he can't fit in a box.

She sees the relief as Hansen steps into the boardroom and then a new dismay when he looks down and through the floor. He gets that under control and spots Signy and Eddie. Ria motions him to a seat and Devan closes the door.

Despite the drumming going on below, the room is quiet now. Signy sees Hansen dying to ask his well-bred, man-of-the-world questions, but Ria stops him by lighting sweetgrass. She offers it to Eddie, Signy, Devan, and Hansen. When it's Hansen's turn, he smudges, self-conscious but pleased. Mostly he's succeeding in not looking at the floor.

When he looks at Ria and Devan, maybe he's realizing that they are part of the culture that grew here. Ria pours bowls of steaming tea. Devan hands it around, starting with Hansen, who cradles the bowl in his hands.

As Devan turns to accept his tea, Hansen looks at his profile, then away, embarrassed. He must have seen Devan's movies, Signy thinks. Then he tries not to stare at Ria. Her dress is the haute couture equivalent of traditional dress, in the softest black leather, with a silver necklace dripping blood-red stones.

He turns to Signy. Once again Astrid has dressed her, this time in an emerald silk suit. Hansen's clearly impressed by their clothes. What was he expecting, prairie grunge?

"I know you must have many questions," Devan says. "As one of the creators of Sunterra Gold, Signy Nilsson will be happy to answer them."

"I'm ready to listen," Hansen says. But he's suddenly off balance, as if this is unknown territory. He's surely been everywhere, lived nearly everywhere. "Dane" must be a courtesy designation for him more than any real allegiance. Still, she sees him having to make an effort to appear at ease.

"Of course everything depends on my seeing your research." He's seen Signy's prospectus but he'll want to see specimens and not just holograms. He'll want pest resistance numbers and protein analysis. She has all that in her briefcase, under the table.

"You will see it, in good time," Eddie says. "Sunterra Gold is everything we've told you. No barbecue, no pretty holograms."

"No fancy rhetoric," Ria says.

"No academic soft shoe," Devan says.

"What I do not understand," Hansen says, "is your timing. I came here to learn about the university's discovery and suddenly there you are."

"I can see why you might wonder," Eddie says. "We weren't planning to market for a few months yet. But the university's pitch changed all that."

"We could go it alone," Devan says. "Just use Sunterra Gold in the west and let it prove out for all the world to see."

"We have a lot of land to reclaim," Ria says.

"But that would take a long time," Devan says. "Years."

Eddie continues. "You represent a unique opportunity. If we don't sell to you now, all your markets will be flooded with

Hybrid 140. And I admit it's a great product. But ours is better. We want the maximum number of people to benefit."

Signy watches Hansen closely. He doesn't seem to question what Eddie is saying, perhaps convinced by his sincerity. Obvious sincerity is one of the things Eddie's good at, whether it's real or not.

"I need to consult with my principals," Hansen says.

"We understand," Devan says.

Signy opens the briefcase, lays materials out on the table. Abstracts, reports, diagrams, tables. She passes them to Hansen, who scans them, one by one.

"It sounds amazing," he says when he's done.

"It's my life's work," Signy says. "Mine and my brother's."

"I'll need to see specimens. Perhaps I could visit your farm? In a few day's time, after I have consulted with my people?"

"Of course."

"So here's our plan," Eddie says, and lays out, logically, economically, vividly, how the three-way partnership will work. A reasonable royalty for Signy and Tomas to ensure that their work can continue and to provide them with the pricey legal representation they're going to need from now on. Unlimited access for the SFNC at cost, but giving Trans-European access to information on their progress and the right to exploit Devan's image in their marketing. A cap on Trans-European's profits to keep the seed affordable and to finance continuing research on new ways to produce food. A fund to help the poorest countries buy the seed. Hansen nods at intervals. Signy thinks they've got him.

5. DRAGLAND'S MEMORY ROOM

Alone with his exhibits, Dragland walks from case to case. Objects appear to hover against the soft velvet: a silver locket engraved with a stylized prairie rose; a plain birch box with dovetailed corners, open to reveal carved combs of sanded, unfinished wood; a bookmark of seven intricately braided strands of handspun wool.

Dragland moves in and out of the vision of a fly motionless on the wall: Eddie's superfly – modified with a solar-powered microdrill on one foot. Over the course of the past week, the fly slowly, almost a molecule at a time, drilled a hole through the window, then let itself into the room. It sends images back whenever a sensor on its head picks up movement. It can also transmit sound.

The night before, it picked up Kuiva, late at night when Dragland was probably asleep. He'd walked through the room, stopping at each of the exhibits.

Twice a day, the fly moves to a new location. It sends back pictures of objects – the wooden box, the silver locket, and the many old photographs. In time it will cover all the exhibits and everything will be known.

On one of the stands sits another cream-coloured box. Dragland opens it and pulls out the soft tetrapacks. He releases the butterflies until they fill the room like a dark snowfall. They fly in and out of the light.

The spyfly can't deal with all the movement. It tries to follow first one butterfly, then another, until the images blur. Its eye is temporarily unable to see.

Dragland steps to the centre of the room and waves his hand in front of him. It triggers an electronic circuit and music plays. Once again a life-size holographic image throbs with light. The golden-haired woman looks alive. Dragland's hand goes out to her, as if he believes she can step from her circle to meet him. As his hand touches the aura of light that laps around her, she speaks.

"Of course I love you, Magnus. I will always love you."

Dragland's eyes fill with tears. The woman's voice is warm, appealing, but the inflections aren't quite right. He brings his hands together in the light. The voice stops, the image fades.

More butterflies settle on him. In a moment his face and throat are clad in monarchs, his hands softly gloved. He stands still as more and more of them land.

Then they begin to die, not one by one, but in clumps. A few cling to his face and hands as if for warmth, but they too succumb, dropping silently away. His eyes search the room, as if expecting to find the reason the butterflies are dying, littering the floor with their lifeless forms. Tears slide down his face. He doesn't bother to wipe them away.

Dragland walks toward the door. He pushes it carelessly aside, screams, and doubles over with pain, clutching his hand.

The fly's eye has adjusted and follows him out of the room.

In the computer room, Kuiva splints and binds Dragland's hand. He administers painkillers. He gives the old man a glass of Laphroaig single malt. When Dragland is calm and reasonably comfortable, Kuiva gives him a slim report.

Dragland reads it, swirling the whiskey in the glass, sipping.

"So," he says, "the new plant is a hybrid and part of its genetic complement comes from grasses that grew here before anyone ever planted wheat."

Kuiva waits, perhaps hoping his work will be praised.

"It's not the whole story," Dragland says. "Clearly the hybrid is well suited to its environment and mere survival is in itself an achievement these days. But it's doing more than surviving. How?"

"It's a combination of the things I suggested," Kuiva says. "Root nutrients, selective breeding to improve the efficiency of photosynthesis, resulting in more moisture being retained within plants...and probably something more."

"I think we'll know what it is very soon."

"I hope so, Mr. Dragland."

"We need more than hope. But don't worry. It's all coming together."

6. NIPAWIN WREKKER COLONY

Signy lands the skyboat on the old road the colony keeps up for aircraft. She sees bush in three directions and the colony buildings and gardens on the fourth, the northern side. The buildings are variations of log cabins, in unexpected, inventive shapes. A postmodern pioneer village.

Signy and Tomas grab their gear from the cargo section and head for the rustic wooden entrance, the quiet settling around them. A warm wind ruffles dusty-leaved aspens. Clumps of cloud drift along through the blue. Songbirds sing. Blue jays screech.

MULTIPLICITY.

So says the burned-wood sign outside the Nipawin Wrekker camp. It's not really a Wrekker camp, Signy thinks, although it does use a lot of recycled materials. It also creates new things.

She loves coming here, watching the way they work. Multiplicity for them means different approaches to problems of survival, a mix of economic activities. It means a variety of people: First Nations, White, Black, Asian. Some have lived their whole lives close to the land. Others never touched dirt until it became necessary for survival. Multiplicity is where she and Tomas might live if they didn't have Sunterra and their work.

Today the grass-fringed streets are empty. Most people will be working in the fields. The handful of children will probably be there too.

Seena's cabin, at the edge of the settlement, is one large room. They go through the unlocked door and stash their stuff. The room is filled with beadwork, quilts, and collections: arrowheads, stone hammers, wooden flutes, herbs and spices in glass jars.

They go out back and look into Seena's garden, where green beans and corn flourish, and wander off to the Meeting Place, which houses a small school, a lab, and a recreation centre. They've got so much to tell her.

Seena's alone in the lab, golden-brown hair loose on her shoulders, brown eyes intent on a microscope slide. Over blue jeans she wears a loose, many-coloured top made of thin strips of fur and leather woven into a warp of tough linen. One of her many crafts, an activity that uses both her cultures. She knows they've come in, but finishes her observation, makes a quick note. Only then does she look up.

"Tomas. Signy. At last."

Seena jumps up and hugs Tomas, and Signy sees the pride on his face, and the anxiety. She thinks he controls these things normally by being a fair distance away from her. Probably can't quite believe he helped create her.

Seena hugs Signy too, her body warm and flexible. She is a wonderful young woman, with her strength and beauty, her intelligence and self-sufficiency.

"Tom," Seena says disapprovingly, "you look tired. You're working too much."

Tomas laughs. He's not used to being scolded by his kid. "You're looking great. Are *you* working too much?"

She laughs. "Nothing I can't manage."

Seena looks so healthy. At Sunterra they're all healthy enough, but with Seena it's like there's a hot spring bubbling inside her.

Seena makes Signy and Tomas get along better. She dulls the competitive edge they have with one another.

When Seena hugged her, Signy felt through the loose top the rounding of Seena's belly. She's going to make Tomas a grandfather. Does Ria know, she wonders?

Seena shows them a report on her new work and its effects at Multiplicity. *Bacterium seenensis* is an organism she discovered in the soil, something no one has seen before. It acts a lot like nitrogen-fixing bacteria, which have been understood for a long time and used to help replenish nitrogen in the soil. But this organism has a different function. Firmly attached to each bacterium is a molecule of water – water it has plucked from the arid atmosphere and conveyed into the soil.

Evaporation is supposed to lead in turn to rain, but rain doesn't necessarily happen if you're in a desert or near-desert. This microbe has come up with a new idea. Don't let the water evaporate. Capture it, draw it down into the soil. When you inoculate plants with the organism, it forms a net covering their outer surfaces. It can also be thought of as a system of ladders to capture the water and lead it back down to the soil.

"Ain't mutation wonderful?" Seena asks.

"Sometimes," Signy says.

"You just happen to find a positive mutation, one which popped up after decades of drought. What are the odds of that?" Tomas wonders.

"But then, given the multiplicity of biological life forms and life processes, why not?" Seena says.

"No reason at all, I guess," Tomas says.

"I want you guys to co-author the paper I'm writing," she says as they watch the microbes growing in cultures. Millions, billions of them.

She takes them to her garden. They examine the corn, the fat ears, the pale golden silk.

"You must have had more rain than we did," Signy suggests. "None of our plots look this good."

"We did have more than you," Seena says. "June was good."

"And of course the bacteria are giving you a micro-climate that's even better." Signy touches the ground: it isn't wet or even damp. But the corn plants are different than the ones in the rest of the garden. Greener; stronger. Seena pulls back the husk along one of the ears to reveal glossy blue kernels of Indian corn.

Tomas smiles. "*Bacterium seenensis*. You're gonna be famous."

"Yeah," Seena laughs. "Dozens of people will hear about me."

"But they'll be the dozens who can understand what you've done. In the meantime, I haven't seen corn like this in fifteen years. All thanks to an enterprising mutant."

An enterprising mutant that's doing the same thing for Sunterra Gold, and has been all summer. That's the one thing they're not telling Hansen or Eddie or anybody. Not until they're absolutely sure things are going to work out.

"I'm growing them as fast as I can, but I'd like to increase production," Seena says. "Tom, I want you to come up and work with me."

Signy watches Tomas consider. Seena can probably do the work on her own. But she wants another like mind with her, a sifting, comparing intelligence. Somebody she knows she can work with. Genetics can often give you that; Signy should know.

"So who's the lucky dad?" Tomas sips a cold beer as Seena makes tea. Signy smiles: Tomas did notice.

Seena blushes. "His name is Sayan. He trains our horses."

"I don't think I've met him."

"He was away at another camp last time you were here. Anyway, we weren't together then."

"Nice guy? Worthy of my daughter?"

"Hand-picked. Smart, sensitive, strong. But gentle."

Tomas surveys the cabin. "I don't see any signs of another occupant."

Seena laughs. "We don't live together, not at this point."

"Gee, call me old-fashioned, but I thought that's what people did when they were having a baby together."

"You probably are a bit old-fashioned," she says. "But I like that in a dad."

Signy laughs. "That's right, make him feel old."

"So how will you manage?" Tomas asks.

"Piece of cake," she says. "I'm young, healthy, and emotionally stable. The whole community will help babysit. We need kids here. Our fertility rate hasn't exactly been soaring."

"I suppose that makes sense," Tomas says.

"I think this calls for a celebration," she says. "So I'm making us a corn pudding."

At that moment, Seena, with her strong body, her capable hands, the expression of wry good humour on her face, looks so much like Ria that it's uncanny. Tomas has to turn away.

"What's wrong?" Seena asks.

"Nothing," he says. "Just now, you reminded me a lot of your mother."

"Oh. Isn't that good?"

"Of course it's good. It reminded me, that's all. I really screwed up there."

"Sorry. Can't help that."

"Oh well, never mind. Does she know about the baby?"

"Not yet. I've been waiting till I was sure everything was okay."

"But you'll let her know soon?"

"Don't worry, I will. Now it's time to cook. You can chop vegetables."

Tomas stands still while Seena ties an apron around his waist.

"Oh...Seena," Signy says. "This is so..."

"Fabulous," Tomas says. "Sumptuous."

"Luscious. Sensuous." Signy can hardly bring herself to swallow. The corn pudding is splendid. It has eggs in it: they have chickens here. It has butter: they have milk cows. The rich, grainy custard satisfies in a way she can't remember feeling for a long time. Seena eats like a lumberjack. Or a thresher.

"Probably just like your great-grandmother used to make in the old Swedish Colony," Seena says.

"I'm not sure she knew about corn pudding," Tomas says, "but she would certainly have approved."

"So how's your work going? You must be just about wrapping it up."

Signy can see exactly what she's thinking. Sunterra Gold is a fact. Signy could finish gathering the data herself and Tom could come to the camp and work with her.

"Maybe I could come help you," Tomas says. "For part of the year, anyway."

"That would be great," Seena says.

"The truth is, I expect to have more time soon. It looks like we could have a buyer."

The door opens and a man comes in, a short man with a strong build. He has thick black hair to his shoulders and a black moustache turned down at the corners. He looks like Siberian people Signy's seen in pictures. For a moment he is taken aback, then he smiles, as if the sun shines out of his face.

"This is Sayan," Seena says.

"You are Seena's family," Sayan says. "It's good to meet you." He shakes their hands in turn, kisses Signy's cheek. He treats her and Tomas with the most amazing openness. She doesn't remember anything like it, or not for a long time. Even Tomas relaxes.

"Sayan is from Tuva," Seena says as she sets a place for him.

"You know of Tuva?" he asks. "There's only a few hundred thousand of us in the world."

"Yes, I do," Signy says. "I love Tuvan throat music." She has several albums, and after long practice, has taught herself to chant a note with a clearly discernible overtone.

"We have good songs," Sayan says. "Most of them are about riding horses. Or about our girlfriends."

"But mostly horses," Seena says, and the two of them laugh. "I mean, it's only natural, they spend more time with the horses."

Sayan tucks into the corn pudding with an appetite that matches Seena's. After a bit he looks up, touches her face, and says, "It's good, sweetheart." He winks at Signy. "Working with horses teaches you how to talk to a woman."

"Sayan is named after a range of mountains in the north of Tuva," Seena says. "You can see them in the distance where his people live."

Signy is dying to ask why a man from a small country near Mongolia came all the way to Canada. He guesses her question, his dark eyes amused.

"I heard you had a most beautiful country here," he says. "I've been all over. The Big Muddy, the Missouri Coteau, the Great Sand Hills. This is a great country. Like Tuva. It has strong spirit."

Signy shivers. She could tell him about the times she lies down in the grass and feels the grass and the earth calling to her. She could tell him about her rounds and the leaving of water and tobacco. He would understand.

"Many people tried to kill their land," he says matter-of-factly. "But it's not dead."

"No," Signy agrees, "it's not."

After dinner Tomas talks about their troubles with Dragland, especially the attack on David. Signy can't resist phoning home, where Astrid is staying with David. Astrid teases her about checking up on them, but it's not often that both Signy and Tomas are away.

"Maybe you should all move up here," Seena says. "We could certainly use you. And I'd have three more babysitters."

"We'll see," Tomas says.

"So," Signy says, "we didn't just come up to see how your work's going. There's a lot happening and we thought you needed to know." Signy tells Seena and Sayan about the decision to work with Devan and Ria. And about Torben Hansen and Trans-European Foods AG.

"Are you crazy?" Seena asks. "You can't sell to Trans-European."

Signy feels a nasty lurch in her midsection. "Why not?" she asks.

"Come here." Seena leads Signy to the computer. "I'll show you."

Seena begins to search the Web, her hands flying over the keys. She uses a common search engine to call up information on Trans-European and its parent companies Transcontinental Environics and World Bio-Enterprises. She lists several of their smaller subsidiary companies.

"I did all that," Signy protests.

"You don't understand," Seena says. She types in the name of one of the smaller companies and gets a brief, banal printout. Then she enters a complex alphanumerical code. A question appears requiring her to confirm her identity, and she enters another code, and so on until a video of a sun going supernova fills the screen. It fades and reveals a cache of information.

"The information you need is encrypted," Seena says. "If you can crack it, it tells you everything you want to know."

"How...?" Tomas asks.

"Friend of mine showed me."

"Someone here?" Signy asks.

"We have a cool computer guy. There's various mathematical formulas you can try to work out their codes. He showed me how."

"He's a hacker?" Signy asks.

"More than that. He learned a lot from hackers. Now he's just part of our operation."

Seena continues asking questions, taking the subsidiary up the family tree of ownership. It stops when she gets to Universal Development and demands more codes. She pauses to think for a while. "You don't want to get it wrong," she says, "that might alert their security people."

Slowly and carefully she types in a new code and again the supernova fills the screen. When it fades, the answer is clear. There's one more tier above them all: Dragland Enterprises.

"Jesus!" Tomas says.

Well, it had to be that. Why hadn't they thought of calling Seena in the first place?

"Don't say it," Signy says to Tomas. "I got dressed up in green silk to try and sell our life's work to Dragland."

"But there's no deal yet?" Seena asks.

"No," Tomas says, "and there won't be one."

"Let's look a bit further," Seena says.

Seena requests a listing of all holdings of Dragland Enterprises. The general outline is similar to what they knew before, but there's much more detail. Dragland owns not just corporations and land but lakes, rivers, cities, universities. How could even a computer keep track of all this? How could anyone go about their daily life knowing they own all this? How could they breathe knowing it?

Signy stares at the screen, her body icy cold. All the paranoia she's been suppressing lately is back. She remembers stories that used to circulate, urban myths, people said, about big automakers buying up patents to cheaper, safer engines, and then making sure they were never built. Wilder stories suggesting that inventors who didn't play ball ended up dead. Nobody'd believed these stories, not really. She realizes that human brains and emotions aren't equipped to deal with anything like Dragland Enterprises.

How could you make any agreement with an entity like this? How could you ever enforce their part of the agreement?

She's been so used to thinking of herself and Tomas as having a measure of power. Influence. Allies. Independence. The best intellectual property lawyer in the country. They do have these things, but she sees now how small the area is where they have them.

Why had she listened to Eddie?

"Signy, what's the name of that guy you're dealing with?" Seena asks.

"Hansen," she says. "Torben Hansen."

Signy and Tomas had looked him up before, but with Seena's codes his connections to Dragland become clear. He got his start working for the Magnus Foundation, Dragland's charitable entity. Doing Dragland's clean work for him. But there's so much more.

Seena traces Hansen's movement through the vast, all but organic structure of Dragland's domain. Hansen has been nourished, rewarded, promoted, to become the handsome golden face of everything about Dragland you can't see.

Hansen has brought in so many properties, made so many deals. He must be Dragland's favourite operator. He buys up companies, funds research stations, creates new management structures. He specializes in new products that may have a significant effect on the environment. She can hardly take it all in.

Then, embedded in the nearly endless list of companies, she spots something else: Baikalpur.

"Tomas, he owns Lake Baikal."

"What? Where?"

She points. "He owns Lake Baikal. Like it was a thing."

"You can't own Lake Baikal," Sayan says. She'd forgotten he was there.

"No," she says, "look. Baikalpur. That's the company that's going to sell the water."

"You can't own it," he says with certainty.

Thomas reaches in his pocket for his phone. He dials and after a few rings someone picks up. "Eddie," he says, "we can't sell to Hansen... I know... I know. But we can't. His company is part of Dragland Enterprises... Yep, it *is* a bitch. Gotta go... Yeah. Bye."

That night Seena's cabin is cool enough for her to light her fireplace. The four of them sit drinking spiced chai.

Signy tells Sayan about the Sand Castles, which he's never seen. They talk about going to see them in the fall. They talk about going north to fish on the Churchill River. She describes Nistowiak Falls, which he's never seen. Lake Athabasca.

"I've seen Lake Baikal," Sayan says. "It's not far from my country."

"I'd love to go there," Signy says. "The world's biggest lake."

"It is the world's biggest lake," he agrees. "But that's not why I said that man can't own it." They wait for him to explain.

"The lake is twenty-five million years old, and it has a life of its own. Someone may have signed papers that say this man owns it, but I think that will not be the last word. I think the people will speak and I think the lake will find a way to speak also."

"I hope you're right," she says.

"Do you think that much water, more than in all your Great Lakes put together, is just sitting there these twenty-five million years? Do you think it has no thoughts of its own?"

No one answers. "Do you know the legend of Khori Tumed?" he asks. "My mother told it to me."

"Tell us," Seena says.

"You may know that there's an island in Lake Baikal, called Olkhon, and fishermen live there. It's seventy kilometres long, big enough that it has many small lakes of its own. Long ago, on the island of Olkhon, a man called Khori Tumed saw nine swans fly through the air and land on the island. As he watched from a grove of birch trees, their dresses of feathers fell from their bodies and they became nine beautiful women who bathed naked in the lake. While they played in the water, Khori Tumed stole one of the feather dresses and buried it. Then when the swan women put on their feathered garments, only eight could fly away. The ninth remained and married Khori Tumed."

Signy feels a thrill. Surely it was wrong for the man to steal the swan feathers, and yet he must have wanted the woman so much.

"They lived together, very happy, and the swan woman gave him eleven sons. Sometimes she would ask about her lost feathers, but Khori Tumed would never tell her where they were. And then, years later, a day came when she asked again. She said she wished to try the feathers on one more time.

"She reasoned with him, assuring him she would not be able to escape, since he could easily bar the door of their yurt.

"And Khori Tumed listened to his wife's yearning and he believed no harm could come of such a thing. So he brought the feathers, and his wife tried them on. Suddenly, a swan once more, she flew up to the smoke hole of their yurt. Khori Tumed reached after her, and managed to grab her feet. He wept and begged her to stay, at least long enough to name their sons.

"You understand?" Sayan asks. "The custom was that each son was named when he reached manhood." They nod.

"Because Khori Tumed had listened to her deepest wish, his swan love heard his. She stayed until all the sons became grown men. Khori Tumed at last agreed that she should go. Once more she put on her dress of feathers. She circled the yurt, blessing him and their sons, then flew away, once more a graceful swan."

Signy saw it all, the swan woman flowing back into her feathers, finding once again her true nature.

"For years," Sayan says, "I thought the story was about my mother, but I was afraid to mention it. I kept searching for places where her feathers might be hidden, but I never found them. One day she asked me why I looked sad and I told her. She said she was sorry I was worried, that it was just an old tale. But see, I never forgot the story."

Tears run down Seena's face. "Must be my hormones," she says, but they all know it isn't that.

Next afternoon, Sayan has taken Tomas hunting and Signy is helping Seena in the lab when her sat phone rings.

No one there. A text message snakes down the screen. "Astrid's hurt. Dragland's plane sprayed us with poison. Most of it got on Astrid. Her tongue is swollen and she can hardly breathe. She's got red blotches. What should I do?"

"David," she writes, "get the Anakit from the medicine cabinet. Give Astrid a shot. Do you understand?" His words appear: "I understand." "Good," Signy writes. "If you get symptoms like Astrid's, give yourself a shot. In the meantime, if you can swallow, take two antihistamine pills with water, same as you do when you have allergies. If you think Astrid can swallow and not choke, you can dissolve the pills in water and give her some too."

"I understand," he replies. "Come."

7. KUIVA'S ROOM

"Why on earth would you want to leave?" Dragland holds up a handwritten letter which has been crumpled and then smoothed out again.

Kuiva doesn't answer.

"What were you thinking? You left me on my own just when I needed you, when I was in pain."

Kuiva moves to the corner furthest away from the door and sits on a leather chair, his face still as stone.

"I can overlook that, of course, but what does this mean? You've given no warning, no hint – " Dragland stops, puzzled about how to approach the problem.

Kuiva's room in the Dragland compound is spacious, self-contained, with areas for eating, sleeping, relaxing. A spaceship for one. Everything is soaked in shades of blue and grey with a touch of green: teal blue walls and ceiling, low upholstered benches in slate and spruce. Crystal objects perch on clear glass shelves: elegant birds, so stylized they are more the idea of birds; shimmering vases; large abstract pieces like chunks of glacier ice.

"Why would you want to leave, just when we're making headway? Just when we're going to win!" Kuiva meets Dragland's eyes. The question, "We?" hangs in the air.

"You have so many advantages."

Kuiva looks at the old man as if to ask, What advantages?

"You have personal security, in a way few people in this world do. Safe food and shelter, and protection from your enemies."

"I don't have enemies," Kuiva says. "I don't have enough of a life to have made any."

Dragland ignores this. "You have a position of trust most people could not even imagine. You have princely financial reward, although admittedly there's not much to spend money on around here. Still, there will always be luxury mail order catalogues. I can see the results all around this room."

He touches a palm console and coloured lights swirl across the room, simulating the aurora borealis, drenching the walls and ceiling with shimmering colour, sparking rainbow colours in the glass pieces.

He waits for Kuiva to acknowledge what he's saying, but Kuiva says nothing. "You have interesting work," he goes on, "with the resources to create nearly anything your mind can imagine." Kuiva takes one of the ice-chunk sculptures in his hand.

"You have air conditioning. Who has that nowadays? More amazing, you have all the water you could ever want."

Finally Kuiva ventures something. "Not if you've seen the ocean. Polar ice caps. Northern lakes."

"You know I don't object to a fishing trip or two. You could even visit Sweden if you gave me enough notice. You could visit the Saami, your people."

"I don't have any people. Anyway, I always have to think of your bones. What if you broke a bone?"

"I could manage," Dragland says, unconsciously touching his splinted hand. "I could be extra careful. It's not like I break a bone every day."

"Tell me," says Kuiva, "how long were you thinking I would stay?"

"I don't know, there has never been a definite time limit. I suppose I thought it possible that you would stay on until... That you would stay as long as I needed you."

"I see," says Kuiva, "and then?"

"And then you'd make new arrangements. How do I know what you're going to want to do at a hypothetical time in the future?"

"You're right. How could you possibly know that?"

"Look here," Dragland says, "is all this because you don't think I acknowledge your abilities?" Kuiva is silent. "Because I do, you know. Of course I do."

Kuiva turns off the northern lights.

"You designed and supervised the building of our solar stills. Our soaking pool. Our sauna. That was...excellent. You built my spy-eyes." No response.

"You arrange for every single thing we eat or wear or work with. I had thought you liked it." Nothing.

"You coordinate my communications with all my managers and enterprises throughout the world." Now Dragland waits.

"What am I to you?" Kuiva asks. "Colleague? Employee? Servant?"

"Of course you're my employee. What's wrong with that? What's wrong with any of this?"

"It's ten years now since I've lived in the world."

"When your work here is finished, you can go back to Sweden, buy a fine home. You can have people work for you. You could even go north and try to recreate the life your people once had."

"As futile as that would be," Kuiva says softly. "And I could take back my real name. The one you made me change."

Dragland looks embarrassed. "Well, who would believe a Saami with a Finnish name?"

"It's very common," Kuiva says. "People marry outside their ethnic group all the time."

"The point is, it was hard to pronounce, with, what was it, fourteen letters, most of them vowels. Most of them double vowels, in fact." Dragland gives a jovial laugh, as though he's been exceptionally witty. "Kuiva suits you much better," he insists, "and it does have a sort of Finnish or Lappish sound to it."

"I have no time I can say is my own. I have hours when in theory I do not work. But you can snatch them away at any moment. I might as well belong to a feudal lord."

"Oh, is that the problem?"

Kuiva shakes his head. "I have nothing of my own. Nothing in this room reflects my past. I have no family photographs or mementoes. No recorded music, no well-read books. It's not like that for you. Everything here has a meaning for you."

"And so it should for you," Dragland says. "I've given you a place in my home. You were getting nowhere when I found you in Uppsala – in a job that used one tenth of your talents. I saw what you could do when the university didn't. You were nothing before."

Kuiva takes a deep breath. "Is that what you wanted? A person who was nothing?"

"Don't be a fool," Dragland says. He reaches out a hand to steady himself and touches the palm console again. The walls and ceiling become a world of ice, peaks and ridges and distant ranges of ice, the two men in the centre, as if someone had placed comfortable furniture in the middle of a glacier.

Dragland is pleased with the illusion. "I didn't know you were interested in glaciers," he says, as if he's forgotten the discussion underway.

"They're like the northern lights," Kuiva says. "They call to me."

"Yes, of course, they're fascinating."

"They're not just dead ice," Kuiva says.

"What?" Dragland asks, embarrassed.

"Many organisms live in the ice."

"Of course, but – "

"Think of the hours, days, centuries they've existed," Kuiva says. "Think of their slow, patient deposition and compression. The grinding, smoothing weight scoring the land. The slow dance across mountains. Think of streams, lakes, rivers of ice. Deep, still rivers, sleeping perhaps, or dreaming; always waiting.

"Well," says Dragland, "that's the longest speech I've ever heard you make. Very fanciful."

"'Think of them as rock,' one of my professors said, 'only they have a lower melting point.' When he said that, he didn't know they were going to melt in his lifetime."

Dragland sneers. "Are you turning into an environmental zealot? Is that what this is about? In any case, we can continue this another time." He heads for the door.

"I don't remember what I've told you about my people," Kuiva says, and the old man stops. "It's true, of course, that I don't have any, either in the sense of immediate family or of a single ethnocultural group. My mother was Saami, my father Finnish and Swedish. My father died in a logging accident when I was a baby. My mother died, I don't know of what. I was a small child in a cold city."

"Yes, I know. You were adopted by that scientist, that geneticist."

"Professor Sundstrom was good to me. He saw that I had abilities in science and engineering and he made sure I had a good education."

Dragland inches toward the door. "I have things to see to – "

"His wife and daughter were good to me too. In the way you might be good to a valued pet that can learn tricks beyond anything you ever imagined."

"For God's sake, man, get a hold of yourself. I don't have any family, and you don't hear me carrying on. My people have been dead seventy years."

"When the professor died, I couldn't stay on with Ulla and my 'sister' Kati."

"I have to check the monitors," Dragland says. "Don't you understand? I've finally acted. Set things in motion. I won't fail this time."

"I worked hard at the university, but all the time, deep down, I was waiting for someone to come for me. What did you see in me? What were you looking for?"

"All right, if you insist. I was looking for someone with scientific brilliance who would do what I asked without tedious questions. Someone who would come and stay a long time and be missed by no one."

"I see." Kuiva won't meet Dragland's eyes.

"Mostly, I wanted someone who would help me." This last part surprises Dragland. "And you have helped. You've done all I could have asked."

The words are too late. Kuiva doesn't speak, and after a moment, Dragland can't bear the silence. He walks out the door.

PART SIX

THOR'S HAMMER

I. SUNTERRA FARM

Signy makes the flight in just over an hour. She finds Astrid lying on the sofa, the skin on her face and arms swollen and covered with lesions, but conscious. David sits beside her, holding her hand. Thank God, he looks all right, except for red weals on his hands and forehead. He's sleepy, probably from the antihistamines. He must have forced himself to stay awake. She bends to hug him, touches her cheek softly to his.

"Have you both had water?" she asks. David nods. He slumps back in the easy chair.

Astrid tries to smile. Signy examines her tongue: swollen, but not enough to prevent swallowing. Her breathing is good. Signy pats her hand.

She's already talked to a poison and allergy specialist in Saskatoon. She can give more antihistamines in a few hours. If they have nausea, she can give them Gravol. If either becomes unconscious or has difficulty breathing, she has to bring them to Saskatoon to the hospital. As if that's going to help if they die on the way. Otherwise, she might as well keep them there. Keep Astrid on fluids for a while.

David has fallen asleep in the chair and Astrid's eyes are closing, as if they feel safe, now that Signy's here to help.

"That's right," Signy says, "sleep now."

She watches them for a while, then puts the kettle on for tea. She calls Seena to let her know they're okay. Seena expects Tomas and Sayan back later in the evening.

As the kettle comes to a boil, Signy starts to sob. She could have lost them both.

Several hours later, Astrid is fully conscious. Although she's still weak, her tongue is almost back to normal size, but covered in red bumps. She drinks a glass of water.

Signy gets tea for them both and pulls up a chair by the sofa. Astrid reaches for her hand.

"It's okay, Sig. None of this is your fault."

Signy looks at Astrid, at the face so like her own. Why am I so afraid of her? she wonders. She's always hated having to see this other version of herself. *A better version.* Maybe she could let that go.

"I'm sorry things didn't always go well between us," she says. "I can be a bit of a bitch, can't I?"

"A bit?" Astrid laughs, but Signy can see it hurts her tongue. "Ancient history," she says. "You've been nicer lately."

David wakes and asks for tea. His tongue is nearly normal.

She gives him sweet milky tea, not too hot. As he sips it, she feels a sense of deliverance. David's safe, and Astrid will be too.

"What were you doing?" Signy asks David.

"I took Astrid walking on the home quarter."

"He wanted to see if I could hear the music." Astrid smiles. "All I could hear was the wind, and a sort of hum in the grass. Oh, and a sparrow. You don't get many birds now, do you? But sparrows always seem to hang on."

"I could hear it like always," David says, "like a river, moving all the time. Then it...slipped."

"I heard a small airplane. I saw it coming. There was no pilot. No cockpit even," Astrid says.

"A drone," Signy says. "He uses them to spray his crops."

"I felt a fine mist on my face and saw clouds of it all around me." Astrid looks terrified now that she's reliving it.

"Easy," Signy says, "it's all right."

"I pushed David to the ground, tried to cover him, but I know it got him in a few places. Signy, if I hadn't known it was poison, I'd have thought it was rain. Soft, cool rain."

"I hate him," David says. It's the most emotion she's ever heard in his voice. She touches his face.

"It's okay," she says. "It's okay now."

After supper for herself and David and broth for Astrid, they sit quietly, Astrid propped up on pillows on the sofa. Soon David goes to bed.

Signy gets fresh tea for herself and Astrid. They sit comfortably in the darkening room. Signy remembers the discovery she made in the attic when they were working on the train.

"I found some papers of Solveig's you might like to see," she says. "In the attic. Under the lining of the trunk."

"Let's have a look."

Signy hesitates. "You never know what to expect with Solveig. She can be unsettling."

"She wasn't just our great-grandmother, you know. She had a life."

"So you feel up to it?"

Astrid nods. "You bet."

Signy undoes the ribbon and begins sifting. She hands things to Astrid – recipes, old birthday cards, old letters – plain, utilitarian communications about births, deaths, illnesses. Baby pictures of Tomas, Signy, and Astrid. At the bottom of the pile, she finds one longer letter.

"Look at this. A letter written to your mom."

"What's it doing here then?" Astrid asks.

"I don't know," Signy says. "I guess it was never sent." She examines it for clues. "It's dated September, 1990. She would have been eighty-nine." She holds it out to Astrid.

"You read it to me. I'm too tired."

"All right."

Dear Mattie,

Today a nice young man came to see me (Jason Karlsson, Bertil's son). Some people are getting together to compile a local history of the Swedish Colony. They want me, as the oldest surviving lady, to give them my story. I'm to start at our first homestead in the south country and then tell about coming north to the colony. My story and this book will be a legacy to our descendants.

I know what they want to hear. How can I tell them the truth about any of it? Start at the homestead? I wanted nothing so much as to leave those endless parched hills. The incredible vistas everyone went on about. The hundreds of miles of the same thing.

I suppose there was beauty in it. The trouble is, there was more than you could stand. At times I could swear the hills talked to me. "We don't need you. Nothing here needs you." I wanted less beauty and more people around me.

"After all," Astrid interrupts, "she came from a place with lots of trees. The Dirt Hills would have been quite a shock." Signy continues.

Be careful what you wish for, my mother used to say. We did leave, along with most of the neighbours who came with us from the Old Country, because there was no choice. It was a blazing hot day in 1933. I was thirty-two years old.

Everybody said the new Swedish Colony would be just what we needed. Rolling hills, good soil, aspen bluffs in the coulees. We would be new pioneers, in a place where it still rained. And it did seem as if time had rolled back and things were still green and hopeful. Birds sang all the day, orioles and redwings and robins.

They were lovely farms. Swedes all over the place, with the occasional Norwegian, and all of them so glad to be here.

"Oh, it's so much more land than we could ever have had in the Old Country."

"Oh, the rain is so dependable, and our crops grow so well."

"Oh, it's lovely to be here with our own people."

Astrid laughs. "They were still saying that when we were young."

I wanted to scream: "Oh, it's all so bloody lovely!" People would have been shocked. Women aren't supposed to swear. And I never did in the Old Country, where things were supposed to be so bad!

I'm sick of Swedes, that must be it. Swedes say Norwegians are just Swedes with their brains bashed in. Maybe it's the other way around.

It took me many years to figure out what I'm telling you now. If only I'd worked it out sooner. Why did we come all this way to create a Swedish colony? I sure didn't come all this way to remake Sweden. There already is a Sweden, and apparently we all thought it would be a damn good idea to leave it.

When I was a child, Father took us to visit his relatives in Stockholm. My cousins wore different clothes than I did and played different games. Their parents made them include me, but I could see what they thought. Look at the country kid. We have to play with her, but we don't have to like it.

"Ah!" Astrid says. "This is where it all started. She wanted to be like the cousins."

"No," Signy says, reading ahead, "it's not that simple."

I didn't just want what they had. I wanted life to be more interesting. I wanted people to talk to me in a respectful way. People of all kinds, not just Swedes.

I wanted to wear soft, flowing dresses and live in a house filled with beautiful colours and satiny, glowing fabrics. I wanted friends, men and women, strong, kind people who could talk about many things.

What did I get? Feeding chickens, milking cows, weeding potatoes and turnips and cabbage. Canning, berry picking, cooking, sewing, knitting, embroidering. Washing clothes until my hands were cracked and red. Killing and plucking the disgusting chickens and the ducks Baldur shot.

God, how I hate ducks. And chickens. And surely it was never so cold in our old valley near Torsby.

Was there a moment when I had any kind of choice? I could surely have been a farm wife's hired girl. Or maybe I could have gone to normal school and taught in a one-room school. Or learned to type and worked in an office. And I didn't even try!

Signy stops. Up until now, her great-grandmother stayed comfortably in the past. Now she's pulling the stuffing out of her nice old grandma image.

"Might as well finish," Astrid says.

Everyone thought I was happy. For heaven's sake, I had Baldur, the best-looking man in the colony, just like the old story. You know, I used to wonder if Loki is just this fellow who's not very nice or if he's meant to be inside us all.

I must admit, I was exaggerating earlier. Of course people complained. When the rain didn't come, when the sun burned the land to dust. That didn't happen often in the colony, just enough to remind you. Loki is out there.

People also complained about the mosquitoes and grasshoppers. And the hail. And the blizzards. And the roads. And the taxes. And the government. And the floods, but floods hardly ever happened. Just often enough. Loki.

Why couldn't I be like other women and learn to make the best of it?

I know what I have to write for the young man. Praise the sunrises and the sunsets. The hard work that brought a better life. The pleasure in knitting scarves and sewing quilts. The opportunities for our children. The clean, fresh air. The good people.

I could write down all these things. But Loki's got hold of me. I see him creeping around, looking in the window, planning to burn down the haystack. What the hell's the matter with me?

Of course I'm only guessing that other women made the best of it. What if they all felt this way?

Oh, damn it, Mattie, I don't feel like writing all that sweet old lady stuff. I had trouble keeping that up after your grandfather died. Maybe I'll write about Loki instead, how he's always out there waiting, so you better look out.

Or maybe I'll skip the whole thing. Have a shot of aquavit and take a nap. I can tell Jason I really can't remember much. Poor old lady, he'll think.

Sorry to make you listen to an old woman's grumbling. You'd wonder how someone could grumble who had such wonderful granddaughters! Even when you girls got in trouble – when didn't you! – you were still wonderful. Come and see me and I'll give you coffee and those sweet cakes you like. My best love, Grandmother Solveig.

"Wow," Astrid says. "So much for the pioneer experience. The devoted matriarch."

"They must have existed," Signy says. "I used to see it all the time in the obituaries. 'Pernilla loved to cook and sew for her family.' 'Gun loved her family and her garden.' 'Mai was a wonderful knitter and her embroidery was known throughout the colony.' I used to be glad they'd never be able to say any of those things about me."

"You know, Sig, I like her better this way. Sort of takes the heat off, you know?"

"She wasn't perfect, so we don't have to be."

"Must be a relief for you," Astrid says. Signy wings a cushion at her.

"I think I could have a little brandy now, if you have any," Astrid says. "To help me fall asleep."

As Signy pours, Tom calls. It's a relief to hear his voice. Seena's filled him in on what happened. He'll be back early tomorrow. She sits down by Astrid with the brandy, but Astrid is already asleep.

Signy awakens in the night and realizes something's not right. Astrid is still sleeping on the sofa, but when she runs to David's room, he's gone. She remembers his words: "I hate him."

"Christ," she whispers. She should have been suspicious when he went so meekly to bed.

She touches Astrid's shoulder. "Astrid," she says softly, "wake up."

Astrid opens her eyes, confused.

"David's gone," Signy says.

"Gone where?" Astrid grabs the back of the sofa, tries to sit up. Signy lets her put it together. "Dragland's? How would he get there?"

"Must have walked," Signy says. "We haven't fixed that fence yet. If he went through there, it's just a couple of klicks."

"But why go there?"

"To confront Dragland? Make him stop doing things to us? Something like that."

"What are you going to do?"

"If I take the skyboat, maybe I can head him off. I have to leave you alone."

"Just go! I'll be fine."

Signy changes to her jumpsuit. In the kitchen she grabs a flashlight and throws a plaid flannel jacket over her shoulder. She takes a set of keys from a hook in the kitchen.

"Hurry!" Astrid calls after her. "But be careful."

Outside it's cool enough for the jacket. In the distance, forked lightning splits the sky. Thor having fun with his hammer, maybe wanting to break the boredom with a grass fire. Please, not tonight, Signy asks.

In the shed, she starts the Valkyrie and taxis out onto the road leading away from the farm. She throttles up the engine and flicks on the lights. Speeds down the road until she can take the boat up gently. She hopes she can make it without crashing into a hill.

She flies over the route she thinks he might have taken. Over the ripe Sunterra Gold and the virgin grassland. Walking this way he would hear their music. She passes over the broken fence to Dragland's land: barren, deadened ground; no music here.

She knows she's close to the compound. She sees a dark hill, clears it, and sees a dull glow leak out around the few lit windows in Dragland's place. The main building is black-walled and smooth, like a lump of obsidian. His bunker, they call it, the north wall dug into the hillside.

The road leading to the compound is surrounded by a high steel-and-wire fence. Signy lands on this road, stopping ten metres from the fence. She can't see far in the dark, but there's no sign of David out here. There's a distant rumble of thunder, and lightning stabs the sky.

She walks to the fence, no doubt electrified. She doesn't know what other security devices there might be. There's an intercom on the gate, but she won't have to use it. Someone has already opened the gate. David? Well, he stopped the tractor. But she doesn't want to dwell on that.

She passes into the yard. It's like a sinister farm equipment dealership, full of tractors, combines, and seeders that no farmer will ever drive. All remote-controlled. In the dark they look like giant raptors.

She sees the darkness under her feet, feels suddenly cold in spite of her jacket. David is in Dragland's house with Kuiva and Dragland. She hasn't seen Dragland in the flesh for two years. She shakes with hatred and adrenaline.

The bunker's smooth door has no doorknob, no window, no old-fashioned spyhole, just a video camera protected by a metal cage. Like the gate, the door is open wide enough for a small twelve-year-old boy to pass through.

2. DRAGLAND'S HOUSE

Inside, a great chill enfolds her, as if an immense and cold animal lives here. She walks down a long hall with many closed doors along it. She passes them by, seeking the one that has Dragland behind it.

She comes to a double steel door labeled MEMORY ROOM. KEEP OUT. The door is ajar. She slips through into darkness.

The Memory Room is pleasantly warm. Soft currents flow over her face. She looks around, trying to understand what it is. She's seen it through Eddie's superfly, but never fully appreciated its circular form. David must be here, but her eyes can't find him.

She walks further into the room and a high curved wall lights up. An old photograph is projected there, ten metres tall: a cabin built into the side of a hill. Her cabin. A woman sits outside on a kitchen chair, shelling peas into an enamelled tin basin. Turned to the camera, she squints into the sun.

Signy moves along the wall and more projections appear – moving images, clouds skimming landscape in time-lapse sequences. She recognizes the Sand Castles, and the Big Muddy. How is it he cares about the same places she does?

The image cross-fades into a northern waterfall – Nistowiak – water breaking against rocks into spray fine as smoke, the camera in so tight she feels as if she's in the water. It changes again: the Great Sand Hills, wind sculpting golden-ochre dunes under a sky that plunges and thrusts against the sand.

Farther along the wall, in the faint moonlight from a big circular window, David watches her. She rushes to him, holds him close. They have no need for words. They're here to complete a task.

They walk through the room and examine the glass cases. They contain objects similar to things they have at home. Solveig's things. David moves into the room's centre. His arm triggers sensors and the image of the woman appears, a hologram close enough to touch. Music from the string quartet floods the room. The woman begins to speak. It is Solveig, at the age Signy is now, her hair loose on her shoulders.

In the computer room, using a flashlight and the battery-operated lights of the emergency system, Kuiva tries to restore power to the video screens as Dragland watches, impatient.

"I don't know what happened," Kuiva says. "I'm getting the solar backup going, but I'm having to do it room by room." In a moment, the computer room is filled with soft background light and soon the screens, showing views of nighttime Sunterra, hum quietly.

Dragland sits in front of the screens, their bluish light reflected onto his tight face.

"What did you say to me?" he asks. "Just before the power went down? What was that again?"

"I said you shouldn't have sent the plane. You shouldn't have sprayed them. They're people." Kuiva speaks calmly.

Dragland looks angry, but hesitates. One of his hands, touching the other, splinted hand, trembles.

"Does your hand hurt?" Kuiva asks, continuing to work on the electrical circuits.

"Yes," Dragland says. "It's like a rodent with very sharp teeth has got into it."

"In a moment I'll get the medicine," Kuiva says.

"Never mind. Only morphine would work and I have to be able to think clearly."

"I see." Kuiva sounds unconcerned.

"You're a fool if you think I'm done with them."

Kuiva continues with his work.

"It's just that bitch Signy Nilsson and her pup, you know. No one cares what happens to them." Kuiva doesn't respond. "Understand: I'm going to have their land. It's all in motion, there's no stopping it. I'll knock down their house and bury it. I'll have their secrets, their research. Everything they've worked for. They'll be sorry." Dragland stops as if he can hear how weak the last words sound – the words of a child.

"If you do all that," Kuiva says, "I won't help you."

"You've decided, then? You're going to leave me?"

"Not necessarily."

"You think you'll stay but you'll decide which instructions to follow."

"Unless you'd rather I just leave."

Dragland looks displeased. Then he hears chamber music from the Memory Room.

"Kuiva!" he says sharply. "The Memory Room is to be kept locked at all times!"

"I don't understand," Kuiva says. "It is locked. Always."

They move into the hall, feel gusts of warm air. The outer door stands open to black night. Kuiva hurries to close it, but it pops back open.

"The lock is damaged," Kuiva says. "First we lost power and then we switched to backup. The door was briefly unlocked. It must have blown open. I'll check it later."

They walk toward the Memory Room, Kuiva and the old man. The music grows louder.

Signy waits in the dark, trying to decide what to do. Kuiva and Dragland enter and stop. They see David in the pool of light, but not Signy in the shadows. Dragland is dumbfounded. Probably hasn't seen a child for years, let alone one he's recently sprayed with poison. His face takes on a calculating look.

"Just what I need," he says, "a hostage."

He must expect David to hear, to look up. David doesn't, but Signy's sure he's aware of the two men in the room.

They still haven't noticed her. She waits.

"Look at me when I speak, damn you!" the old man says.

David pivots slowly, examines Dragland and Kuiva by turns. He shows none of the fear Dragland must be hoping for.

"Stop hurting us," he says.

Dragland is discomposed by the odd, flat voice. "You look all right to me."

David turns to Kuiva. "Do you want to hurt people?"

Kuiva's face goes blank. "No."

"Why help him? For money?"

"Let me be," Kuiva says.

Signy creeps closer, avoiding the exhibits and their lights.

"Why?" David asks again.

"Because I was alone!" Kuiva says. Horror spreads over his face, but there's no taking it back.

Dragland stares at Kuiva with revulsion, backs away. He bumps into one of the cases. Screams.

"Your hand – " Kuiva takes a step toward him.

"Don't touch me!"

The lights waver. A thunderclap shakes the room. Like enormous boxcars shunting around a rail yard in the sky.

David walks toward Dragland, who shrinks against the glass case.

"Your hand is hurt," he says.

"Very observant," Dragland says caustically. "Keep away!" David continues to advance. "Keep away, I tell you!" Dragland's voice rises to a querulous whine.

Kuiva reaches out to hold David back, but stops short.

"Kuiva!" Dragland cries hoarsely, as David takes the old man's hand. David is utterly still, his small hands cradling the brittle fingers. After a moment, Dragland's look of fear and outrage turns to awe. David drops the old man's hand and steps back.

"How did you do that?" Dragland asks, flexing the healed hand. Another shock of thunder shakes the room.

"Are you all right?" Kuiva asks.

"Yes. My hand is better."

This is the moment, Signy thinks, when a person, no matter how ill-bred, might say thank you.

"How did you get in here?" Dragland tries to sound intimidating.

David reaches into his pocket. He pulls out the picture he found in the attic, of Solveig as a teenage girl in a yellow dress, her arm around a young man.

"That's mine!" Dragland seizes the picture.

"Solveig belongs to us," David says.

Dragland smoothes the picture. "I'd lost my copy of this one," he says to Kuiva. "I think it's our best."

"You tried to kill the grass," David says.

Dragland still stares at the picture. "Land is for production."

"I won't let you."

"You can't stop me," Dragland says, his eyes still on the picture. His long, gnarled fingers caress the face.

"You sprayed us with poison. You tried to kill us."

Dragland turns on David, his face contorted. "I wish I had killed you."

David's hands touch the sides of his head. "Stop," he says, "you're hurting me."

Signy crouches to spring forward, but David moves first. He

takes Dragland's hand in both of his. Dragland can't seem to move as David's eyes go hard and bright.

"No!" Dragland screams, his face distorted. "That noise!" he sobs, "I can't bear it. Make it stop!" Thunder drowns his cries. Kuiva moves to support him.

David drops his hand. "It's you," he says. "That's the sound your thoughts make."

Dragland stares at him. "I will destroy you. Do you hear?"

Signy goes to David, puts her arm around him. Lightning flares through the room, their faces glowing in the light.

Magnus Dragland looks at Signy in amazement. "Solveig?" he says, "you've come back?" His body sags against Kuiva.

"I'm not Solveig."

"Do you think I wouldn't know you?" he insists, amused. Tears start in his young eyes.

"Solveig's thirty years dead. I'm Signy Nilsson. You know me, all right."

Then he understands, tries to cover the moment of confusion. "Of course, you're Signy. Solveig is dead. You're not hurt then. From the spray."

"*I'm* not hurt, you bloody fool. You sprayed Astrid. My cousin."

His face twists. "I meant to get you!"

"I said you shouldn't have done it," Kuiva says.

David goes to the centre of the room and waves his hand. The hologram reappears and begins to speak over the music. "Of course I love you."

"You recorded her voice – stole it and reconstructed it," Signy says. "You had no right."

"I had the best right. She loved me."

"She chose my grandfather, Baldur Nilsson."

Thunder builds to a stunning crash. "Thor's coming to get you," Signy says. "He's had enough."

"Don't be ridiculous," Dragland says. "Thor would be on my side, if he existed."

"An old, dying woman," Signy says. "You took her voice. Made her speak false words."

"They weren't false." But Solveig's voice goes on, the manipulation so obvious that it's painful to listen to.

"The voice is too old," Signy says, "even after your technicians have worked it over. It doesn't match the hologram. And the cadences are wrong."

David steps into the image, his hands reaching out. The music fades. For a moment the hologram glows more brightly, then disperses in jolts of light.

"No!" Dragland shouts. Hard rain slashes against the window, rough music on the glass. Dragland looks immensely old now, shoulders slumped, his face sagging like an old burlap bag. Caved in, withered, breached.

Dragland peers at David. "How could you hear my thoughts? How could you send them back at me?" Signy sees his fear.

David approaches, takes the old man's hand again. "This is the sound of your land. Listen." Dragland tries to pull his hand away, but he can't. His bones won't take it. He cringes and grits his teeth. "Now I'll give you my music...grass...things growing."

"No," Signy says, "don't." But David isn't looking at her.

When Dragland begins to hear it, colour comes back to his face. Tension flows out of him. Dragland groans, but it's not pain. With his long white hair, he looks like a prophet granted revelation.

"The prairie alive?" Dragland asks. "How can that be?"

"The grass was here before we came. Thousands of years. You tried to kill it."

"Management..." he says. "I practised good management."

"Soon you will die – "

"I don't want to die," Dragland says.

"Every living thing dies," David says.

Dragland looks older and smaller than before.

"The grass will take you back," David says.

Signy sees Dragland reach for the rage that's sustained him, but he can't take hold of it.

"Come on, David, we have to get back. Astrid needs us." Signy pulls David toward the door.

"Wait," Dragland cries. "You think she didn't love me, but you're wrong. She promised to marry me, before I went away to university. But when I came home, we quarrelled. She thought I only cared about money."

"She was right."

"Let him speak." Kuiva says.

"She was angry...and she accepted Baldur's proposal," Dragland says. "She married him to spite me. Then she was the one who had to pay."

"She loved him. I've seen their pictures."

"Baldur had a *worm* eating away at his brain. Look at the eyes and you'll know. Baldur the good."

"He *was* good." But no examples of goodness come easily to mind.

"One winter, he was sick with pneumonia. They took him to town, to the hospital. I begged her to leave him and come with me. We made love and we were happy."

"I don't believe you."

"They brought him home a day earlier than she expected. Made old doctor Torsson bring him by horse and sleigh. Baldur came in the door, like a corpse walking." Dragland is no longer seeing anything but that moment in the past.

"He looked at her and me, his eyes so malevolent, and I saw the fight go out of her. I knew I couldn't make her come with me." Dragland looks so devastated that she can't keep her eyes on his face.

"We made love in their bed under her feather comforter. It had a pattern of blue flowers."

"You're lying!" But she's seen that comforter.

"Then how do you think this boy speaks to me? How does he speak mind to mind?"

"You can't be serious!"

"Her third child was mine. Your grandmother was *my* daughter."

Signy feels sick. She tries to believe the things she believed when she entered this room, but can't. David watches, not knowing what to do. He reaches out, touches her hand.

"I didn't understand at first," Dragland says, "that the boy was deaf. I thought he was being insolent. After I heard his voice for a while, I understood. My mother, Anneli, had a voice like that. Deaf from birth. Did you know that?"

Signy can't answer. She has heard of Anneli Dragland. Everyone knew she was deaf.

"Kuiva, I'm tired. Could you help me to my room?" Dragland looks evasive, as if he wants to get away before they ask anything he doesn't want to answer. Kuiva offers his arm and the old man leans on him.

"She didn't forgive you at the end, did she," Signy says. "When you stole her voice. She was old and tired of the whole thing."

Dragland looks too exhausted to walk. Signy feels David's hand in hers as they watch the old man out of the room.

For many minutes Signy has stopped hearing thunder, stopped seeing lightning. Now thunder comes roaring back. Lightning sears her eyes.

3. SUNTERRA FARM

Outside, the first pale light is showing, a grey lustre in the sky. Rain pounds them, more than they've seen for years, as if it's all been saved up. They run for the skyboat, pile into it, teeth chattering, search for dry blankets in the back.

They fly low, skimming the contours of the land, not daring to enter the realm of thunder and lightning. In minutes they see their emergency beacon, pulsating at three-second intervals, washing the farmyard in red light. The house lights are on, all of them.

Signy lands near the house and sees a circle of flattened grass. A helicopter. It must have left before the storm hit.

She stops just in front of the door. Sirens scream and they see, through one of the windows, the red light on the security system.

The security system is no use if they're not home. It's not hooked up to anything in the outside world.

They dash for the open door, rain driving in their faces. Inside, everything's a shambles. The monitor screens are smashed, look like shards of ice. Printouts lie in disordered piles. The hard drives and paper files are gone.

They find Astrid on the floor by the sofa, unconscious but still breathing. She's been beaten. Blood trickles from her mouth. Her breathing is shallow, ragged.

Signy kneels, takes her hand. David drops to the floor and takes her other hand.

"Astrid!" Signy screams. The pulsing yard beacon washes red against the blood on Astrid's cheek.

"Help her!" David shouts.

"I don't know what to do!" Signy wipes the blood away on her own sleeve, but more trickles out.

David keeps hold of Astrid's hand. He must be trying to give energy to her, the way he did with Dragland, but nothing happens. He helped the person who didn't deserve it and now he can't help the one he loves.

Signy realizes that Dragland must have sent people here to steal their work. He must have told them not to worry if anyone was hurt.

The thunder and rain and the wailing siren are so loud it's like the end of the world. She can no longer hear Astrid breathing. She touches the artery in her throat, can't feel a pulse. She tries to clear the airway to give mouth-to-mouth, but there's too much blood. It gurgles in Astrid's throat and then stops.

Signy can't bear to look at David. Astrid is dead.

David puts his arms around Astrid. He makes a harsh, low-pitched keening and at first Signy doesn't know what she's hearing.

Signy's satellite phone rings and she can't suppress a scream. It's Tomas, checking in. She has trouble hearing him. He tells her to turn off the siren and she does. When she says that Astrid is dead, he starts to sob. He keeps asking why. Why did they go to Dragland's? Why did Dragland attack Astrid?

"We told Eddie not to sell to Hansen." She gasps for breath, her teeth chattering. "They must have come right after I left. Before the storm hit. If only I hadn't left her. Tomas, I was so mean to her...before, when she lived with us."

"She knew you loved her," he says.

David sits holding Astrid's hand. He has blood on his shirt. His voice mingles with the noise of the storm.

For a moment Signy's mind spits out the idea that someone has died. Time has stopped moving. The room feels like an old wooden ship tossed on a storm-wracked sea. Thunder and lightning feel completely normal. Days might be passing, or seconds.

"Signy," Tomas asks, "are you still there?"

"I'm here."

"Just keep yourself and David safe. I'll be home as soon as I can."

"All right," she says.

"As soon as I can," Tomas repeats.

Signy puts down the phone. She wishes she could talk with Astrid, see her smile and start to answer. She goes to David, puts her arm over his thin shoulders.

David's face changes, as if something inside pulls at the bones. Sound envelops them: immense, directionless, like the roar of a beast as big as a mountain. The air, suddenly thick, presses their bodies like deep, deep water, as if gravity has increased many times over. The torrent of sound pounds the farmyard. Windows bend and shimmer with the force. They should run for the cellar, but it's too late.

David closes his eyes and clings to Astrid's hand.

In the beacon's pulsing light, Signy see a twister rip through the yard, taking out the barn and barely missing the house, the wind turbines, and the skyboat. A weathered wooden shed explodes, a giant's game of pick-up sticks. Grain bins unravel in shiny spirals, sail past alongside a red combine, a silvery wooden rowboat, an ancient John Deere tractor, a stoneboat old as the farm. All juggled by a titanic hand, then flung beyond the beacon's reach.

It takes only seconds and the roaring fades, the whirling debris floats to the ground. The tornado is headed for Dragland's bunker, she thinks.

"He's going to die," David says, suddenly exhausted. His fingers uncurl from around Astrid's hand. He slumps against the back of the armchair, already falling asleep or into unconsciousness. Signy covers him with a blanket. She closes Astrid's eyes and curls up on the floor by the sofa.

PART SEVEN

THE COYOTE

1. DRAGLAND'S PLACE

Tomas arrives a few hours later and helps Signy and David with the things that must be done. He carries Astrid's body to her bed. He puts the room to rights, tidying papers, picking up knocked-over chairs. He makes them tea and insists they eat. He sits for a long time with David, talking about Astrid. How kind she was, how her love will always be with him.

In the morning light, the three of them survey their wrecked yard. The house stands untouched except for shingles torn off and flung randomly to earth. The sky is silent and clear, the air fresh. It feels like the first day of creation, as if someone needs to go out there and start naming things.

Tomas makes the phone calls that will bring in the outside world. The police. Eddie and Ria. Seena.

In late morning they take off in the skyboat across land battered and torn in a half-kilometre swath to Dragland's place, everything eerily still. Only the soft sound of the motor breaks the silence.

In Dragland's yard, the behemoths' metal skins lie shredded wherever the wind dropped them – on the steel roof (corrugated where it was once smooth), in the yard, in fields half a kilometre away. One of Dragland's hawks circles over the compound. It must have started itself again after the storm. So easy to see now: a touch of the mechanical in its flight. Signy imagines it circling until its battery wears out, then plunging to earth.

The fortress house is shattered in places. Other sections are intact. The main door is open. They enter and move down the corridor, past Dragland's control room, its dead monitors, to the Memory Room.

The steel roof bends in the middle and fails to meet the wall in several places. Most of the room is exposed to the morning sun. The floor is paved in wild mosaics of broken glass. Many of the displays are gone, but here and there artifacts remain. Signy bends to retrieve a hand-carved wooden box, sets it absently on a case.

Dragland lies on the floor, a blanket under him. His hair is wild, his clothing creased and wet. The eyes he purchased at such a price stare at a sky of matching blue. He clutches a creased handkerchief that Solveig embroidered long ago. David stands over him, as if there's a final thing he wants to say or do.

Kuiva sits in a folding chair, not touching Dragland, but with his torso arched over the old man in a protective, comfortable, final way.

He looks up at them, his eyes opaque, black. He wears a plain black singlet and black knitted pants. Smooth kid slippers cover his bare feet.

At first he doesn't speak to them, though accepting their presence easily enough, even amicably. Perhaps they've dropped in to chat about the storm. Neighbours. The old Swedish Colony. Three Swedes and one Laplander.

He straightens a lock of the old man's hair. Reaches and smoothes the eyelids down over the watching eyes.

"It wasn't the storm," he says at last.

"What do you mean?" Tomas asks.

"He died after the storm."

David takes in the words. He wanders off to look at the items lying on the floor, stepping carefully in the mounded glass.

"You mean he was out there," Signy says. "By himself."

"I helped him." Kuiva looks pleased.

"In a thunderstorm."

"He didn't seem to mind," Kuiva says. "The lightning was striking all around, but it never touched us."

"He must have been crazy."

"Not if he thought it was the last time he could do it," Kuiva says.

"Is that what he thought?" Tomas asks.

Kuiva nods. "He'd accepted it. Accepted his death."

"I didn't see any acceptance," Signy says.

"Anyway, what's it to you? You wanted him dead, didn't you?" A moment's anger flashes on Kuiva's face.

"No," Signy says. "I wanted him to stop being such a bastard."

Kuiva turns to Tomas, as if expecting him to be more sympathetic. "I think he wept, but it was hard to tell with the rain streaming down."

"You could have been killed," Tomas says.

"I couldn't leave him."

"No?" Tomas asks.

"I'd been thinking of leaving," Kuiva says, "but things should be done in the right way."

"You were thinking of leaving?" Signy asks.

"Well, yes, but nothing was decided." Kuiva fidgets.

Signy looks at Dragland, the handkerchief clasped in his hand.

Kuiva lowers his voice. "I think he wanted to see the place one more time. Later, we came in here."

"And he just lay down and expired?"

"It was peaceful."

"Peaceful! He'd just set up the robbery of our house. They killed my cousin."

"I don't think so," Kuiva says.

His simplicity almost convinces, but another sort of look crosses his face: a bad thought, quickly hidden. Maybe he didn't know what was coming, but he's putting it together now.

Kuiva sighs. "I think he decided to stop. Just to stop everything. The boy said he was going to die." He sounds quite matter-of-fact.

"The *boy* didn't have to be a genius to figure that out," Signy says. "Not even the richest guy in the world is immortal."

"I did try to tell him that sometimes." Conviction steals into his manner. "He never listened before, but he listened to me at the end." A light of unexpected happiness moves across his face.

"The police will be here soon," Tomas tells him. "Flying in from Saskatoon."

"Police?"

"They want to talk to you."

"Very well, Mr. Nilsson."

"Listen," Signy says, "you seem to be in shock."

"Probably," Kuiva says, but he smiles. He looks quietly mad, but not dangerous.

"He thanked me, you know."

"What?" Signy asks.

"He thanked me for my work. Said I'd done a good job." This is followed by an enormously long pause, as if Kuiva's gone to sleep with his eyes wide open. "I think he was pleased with me."

A look of uncertainty crosses his face, and for a few moments the balance between belief and disbelief shifts back and forth. Signy can hardly stand to look at him. Finally the balance seems to settle on belief.

"I'm sorry about your cousin. I didn't know about the spray plane either, he did that on his own. I told him he shouldn't have. I told him you were people."

"Did you know he sent men in a helicopter to steal our work? Did you know they beat Astrid? She didn't die from the spray, she died from the attack."

"No," he says, his eyes filling with tears, "I didn't know. But I remember he said, 'It's all in motion now.'"

David comes back, a carved tortoiseshell hair ornament in

one hand, a journal with a blue linen cover, muddy and torn, in the other.

For a moment it looks as if Kuiva will claim them, but the moment passes. Signy takes the journal, leafs through it. She recognizes the handwriting before she reads the inscription on the flyleaf: "Solveig Nilsson, her book." It goes back to the time when Solveig and Baldur moved to the Swedish Colony and ends near Solveig's death in a nursing home in Saskatoon. Dragland must have stolen it when he taped her voice. As she lay dying.

Signy goes to the end. The final entry is streaked and torn, but she can read it.

Why must I think about any of this any more? My life seems a pattern of mistakes, a crazy woman's quilt, every piece awry in some small way barely noticeable to the casual eye. Clashing colours, the wrong sort of stitching, small sections beginning to unravel.

Thank God I can be alone at last, in a city, where I always wanted to be. I can hardly bear to remember how that man wrecked my life, destroyed my happiness. What did he finally want with me, except to control me, the way he wanted to control everything? I refuse to utter his name again.

If only I could forget his eyes. Why didn't I see the madness until it was too late? Not madness one can pity and excuse, but madness willed and exulted in. Was he born with that will to unravel, to hurt, to break? I will never know.

Loki. Loki. Loki.

Signy reads through to the end, hatred of Dragland growing with every word, and then a pattern shifts in her mind. Solveig is not talking about Dragland. She's talking about Baldur.

She looks around the room, feels as if it's spun on an unseen axis. Kuiva has turned to Tomas, as though there are things he should discuss with another man.

"I must take charge," he says. "It's up to me now."

"Is it?" Tomas asks.

"I'll have to let the lawyers know," Kuiva says. "I hope they'll listen to me."

"Sure they'll listen," Tomas says. "They can't ignore a dead body."

"I wonder what will happen to the company."

Surely the question is, "I wonder what will happen to me?" Maybe this is a less painful way of asking it.

Tomas shakes his head as if to show that the workings of giant corporations are not exactly his strength. Signy thinks of vintage television shows where the policeman says, "Don't leave town." No need to say it here.

Signy touches David's arm, nods. She takes his hand and he doesn't pull it away. They leave quietly, with only a glance at the man lying dead.

Outside, the sun rides high overhead, the wreckage of the yard bathed in light. Sun shines on the faces of the Nilssons, on the skyboat and its painted bird wings. The sky looks deeply blue. The land is dark and moist, the air deliciously cool, a rippling stream on their arms and faces.

The hawk no longer flies. Signy longs to hear a robin, a meadowlark, or even a crow, but all is silent.

A piece of steel from one of Dragland's machines, formed by the wind into a great shallow saucer, has trapped rainwater inside. It sparkles in the sun.

Rainwater.

2. HOME QUARTER

It's David who spots the helicopter on the flight back, a dull black machine in a circle of charred prairie. Signy lands the boat nearby and the three of them approach warily.

Up close, the helicopter doesn't look all that bad, except that it's hovering on grass instead of in air. The passenger cabin has buckled on impact, although the three men are still belted in.

Torben Hansen's face, though seared by flames, is still recognizable. All three must have been knocked unconscious when the chopper hit the ground. Otherwise, they might have been able to get out.

David looks at the men. Signy wishes he didn't have to see any of this, but at least he knows that the men who killed Astrid are dead. Maybe he won't have to keep thinking of them.

The Nilssons' computer disks, hard drive, and papers are all burnt, although some parts might still be readable. Two automatic rifles have been flung onto this material.

Around the helicopter, fire briefly flared before the rain stopped it from spreading. It's a mess now, but the grass will shrug it off.

Signy is fascinated by the boiled-looking eyes of Hansen. It's only a few days since she met the man, shook his hand, drank cocktails with him. She can look at him now and see him start to smile. See the well-groomed hand reach for hers. Hear the instant command of small talk in several languages. Maybe he never thought it would come to murder. But why does she want to give him the benefit of any doubt at all?

If Norwegians are just Swedes with their brains bashed in, as Solveig's mother always maintained, then what are Danes? She reminds herself not to get hysterical.

There's nothing for them to do here. Tomas calls them to the boat and Signy flies them home.

Back at the house, the Royal Canadian Mounted Police arrive, also in a helicopter. It drops to earth, its noise stunning as it churns the air like a second, smaller tornado.

It takes a while to clarify the sequence of events for the two cops. To explain why Astrid has burns and signs of allergic response as well as the more obvious injuries from being assaulted. To explain that the helicopter must have left just before the storm. To describe how the tornado struck Sunterra and moved on to Dragland's place. The woman cop in charge of the investigation looks like she's seen it all but is now seeing something else. For a long time, the guy cop can't believe Tomas and Signy ever had anything worth stealing, or at least not in such an elaborate way. But after an hour or so, even he becomes convinced. They take Astrid to the helicopter in a body bag. David watches from the greenhouse doorway.

The police walk to the home quarter by themselves. When they return, they take off for Dragland's place without saying goodbye.

3. SIGNY'S CABIN

Signy lands the boat in front of her cabin, switches off the perimeter fence and goes inside. She doesn't look around the way she usually does, doesn't even see the colours, the furnishings, everything she's placed here for her comfort and pleasure.

She opens a kitchen cupboard and presses the corner of a back panel. It moves away from the adjoining panels. Behind it is a cavity and a small attaché case. She retrieves it and looks inside. Ten micro-disks and a thick stack of papers. A picture of David, when he was a baby. She doesn't know quite why she put the photo there, but she decides to put it back in the hidey-hole.

She closes the case and goes out, locking up, resetting the fence. She sees no wildlife anywhere, not even a coyote.

Signy stows the case in the boat and taxis down the long, sloping hill until, like a glider, the skyboat can no longer resist the upward thrust of the air.

4. HOME QUARTER

David and Signy walk through the home quarter grass, turned sage green since the storm. The wreckage and bodies are gone.

"Do you hear it?" Signy asks.

"Better than ever," David replies. "I wonder if she heard it. Dragland's mother."

"We'll probably never know. She might have."

They've looked in the colony records, but found no information about Anneli, beyond her name and the names of people in her family. Just another Norwegian, they probably thought. Of course, Signy, Tomas, and David are part Norwegian, as it turns out.

She suspects that means their heads are bashed in from both sides of the family tree. There's an old rhyme the Norwegian kids chanted when she was a kid and the Norwegians tried to defend themselves from the merciless teasing they got. She tells it to David.

"Ten thousand Swedes ran through the weeds,

Chased by one Norwegian."

David laughs. Laughter isn't something he does often, but the silly rhyme sets him off.

"I like to think she did hear the music," he says. "It makes me feel less lonely. Probably no one believed her either."

"Tomas and I believe you. Eddie too."

"Now you do." He speaks calmly; not accusing, just noting. "I've decided. I'm going to be a scientist and help you and Tomas. And Seena."

"That's good. I always thought you would."

"Signy, Dragland wasn't happy. After he lost Solveig, I think he forgot how to be good."

"When you own a large portion of the world," Signy says, "I doubt if goodness comes into it any more."

"I want a better life than that."

"You will have," she says. "You'll have people who love you. You'll have Sunterra and you'll have your music."

They watch the grass blow. The wind against their faces is soft, with a hint of moisture.

"Everything moves, Signy. When I walk here, I can feel the earth turn." She nods.

Without conscious design, they walk to the aspen bluff, to the tall spruce tree. Signy takes David's hand and presses it to the rough bark.

"I miss her," he says.

"I know. Me too."

They walk home into the wind, immersed in the subtle air.

5. SUNTERRA FARM

The lawyer can't conceal his distaste for Tomas and Signy and their home. He looks as though no amount of money can compensate him for having to be here. They feel an equal lack of enthusiasm for the lawyer, who has interrupted their planning session on how to rehabilitate ninety-nine new sections of land. Signy decides not to offer tea.

What he has to tell them, Laurens Blixen admits, he would infinitely rather not tell. He has no choice.

Blixen explains that he's spent the last several days untangling the will of Magnus Dragland, and the multifarious system of interwoven entities he controlled, until he thinks he understands it.

His job has been doubly difficult because the Dragland global mass is under pressure. Without Dragland at the helm, the empire is vulnerable. Legal challenges – to the ownership of this part, or the operating strategy of that part – have popped up everywhere, creating work for other lawyers just like himself.

It's an extremely difficult time. A bothersome, vexing time.

"You're making money. Why would it bother you?" Signy wants him to get on with it.

Blixen forces himself to come to the point. A new development has surfaced since Dragland's death, an aberration brought to their attention by Dragland's assistant, known as Mr. Kuiva. He stops, clearly hating to go on.

"What?" Signy asks. "Tell us and get it over with. We've got work of our own to do."

Blixen clears his throat. "Of course we all knew that in the absence of an heir, Mr. Dragland's ownership of ninety-nine sections of the Swedish Colony would pass to the two of you jointly. This is consistent with the original colony bylaws. What we didn't know is that you have another claim. This was revealed in the papers forwarded by Mr. Kuiva." Again he stops, as if hoping to come up with more delays, diversions, or circumlocutions to prevent having to say what comes next.

Tomas and Signy exchange a glance. What is this guy waiting for? He takes a deep breath and draws his shoulders up. He appears to be deciding that a lawyer must do what a lawyer must do, even if it nearly chokes him. They begin to feel infected by his tension.

"What I must now tell you is that Mr. Dragland made a new provision to his will the night he died. He revealed information not previously known, even to himself. He stipulated that Tomas and Signy Nilsson are his direct descendants and the heirs to his entire holdings. Mr. Kuiva has agreed to stay on for as long as you want to help sort things out."

Signy and Tomas are dumbfounded. The implications are unknowably complex. The shock reminds her of the death of her parents in the 2012 flu pandemic. She'd found she couldn't hold herself up, had to lie down on her bed, heavy as stone, and let the world drift away.

Tomas pours shots from a small bottle of aquavit – found by Signy in the Moose Jaw liquor store after she picked up the research notes. For a long time no one speaks. Even one of the world's highest-priced corporate lawyers can apparently recognize a moment when it's better to choose silence.

After Laurens Blixen leaves, in a hoverlimo with a liveried driver, Signy and Tomas sit at the kitchen table and drink. Everything they've known till now is slipping sideways. Is this Dragland's revenge? A way of destroying the life they've preserved and which supports their work? Or did he simply want to pass on his wealth, now that he had someone of his blood to pass it to?

Signy has a fleeting thought of Lake Baikal, deeper, older, than any other lake on earth, but she has to stop thinking about it immediately. It makes her head spin.

When David comes in from his walk, he finds them sitting there, still silent. He decides to start supper. He bashes around the pots and pans and after a while Signy notices and gets up to help.

6. THE SAND CASTLES

Signy can't remember the ascent of the ancient hog's back being quite this strenuous. Of course, it's thirty-five degrees Celsius and she hasn't done any real climbing for a long time. To get here, she's had to walk across a kilometre of rugged hillside, avoiding prickly pear cactus and a rattlesnake. Rattlesnakes didn't live here when Signy first came, but they do now.

The Sand Castles' dull gold spires and turrets thrust against luminous blue sky, their sides deeply eroded and scored by millennia of winds.

A hawk shrieks, a real one, a redtail soaring on a prairie thermal. Signy wishes she could join him even for a moment.

She has to pay attention. She's crossing a narrow ridge and could easily fall. Several times she thought she'd reached the top, but each time there was another peak ahead.

Finally, she's indisputably there, the view incredible on all sides. She sees the South Saskatchewan and the sandy reaches of what was once Lake Diefenbaker, and ranges of river hills on all sides. She's on the spine of the land. Wind strong enough to make her look to her balance whirls and eddies around her, filling the space with a deep thrumming. The redtail rises almost out of sight.

She finds a smooth space on the ridge and sits. She looks around her at the worn, dry hills. It's been a long time since she's felt such joy, untainted by her usual bad habits and thoughts. This is a good place for her, a place that feeds her. The sun is hot on her head, the air dry and sharp with the smell of sage.

Signy lets her mind rest, lets everything flow away. She remembers everything that's happened this summer, but she can move it to one side and study it now.

She hears a swish of movement behind her, feels a minute displacement of air on her neck. She turns and looks into the eyes of a coyote, his head bent so that his eyes look up at her. She is afraid, but there's nothing she can do, no way she can run. He stands so still; his teeth are close to her throat.

He doesn't move, she doesn't move. At last she decides not to be afraid. She looks into the coyote's eyes. "Yes," she says, "I killed Archie, but I didn't mean to. I'm sorry, but I can't change it."

The coyote watches her for a few minutes, then turns and trots away down the narrow top of the hog's back, as casually as if it were strolling the prairie. After a few seconds, it disappears behind a lower peak. She wonders if she imagined it, but either way, she isn't going to worry about Archie again. She doesn't assume that the coyote forgave her or that the coyote was Archie returned to life, but at the same time, she thinks something passed between them, and she's not going to tell anybody else about it.

She remembers the game the colony kids played when she was young, standing on top of a hill. "I'm the king of the castle, and you're the dirty rascal." She no longer feels like the dirty rascal.

Signy opens her backpack and rises cautiously to her feet. She pulls out a plastic bag and opens the top. Reaching in, she feels the ashy grey stuff inside, gritty against her fingers. She pulls out a handful and tosses it over the side.

She opens the bag wider and flings the contents out around her, in as circular a motion as she can manage. The ash floats out on the wind, but its weight quickly carries it back to the scored, nearly vertical sides of the peaks.

Bits of ash cling to her fingers, settle on her clothes. She's still got Astrid on her hands.

It will be a long time before she can remember Astrid without guilt. Dragland sent the spray plane because he mistook Astrid for Signy. His men must have made the same mistake. She'll have to live with it. She does feel better, having made this pilgrimage. Maybe one day a part of her, a part she couldn't acknowledge before, will be Astrid.

Signy pours water on the hard surface of the rock, tucks tobacco into a crevice. She works her way slowly along the ancient ridge back to the waiting hills.

ACKNOWLEDGEMENTS

I want to thank:

My editor, Fred Stenson, for his excellent and thorough advice.

Nik Burton, Karen Steadman, Deborah Rush, Duncan Campbell, Joanne Gerber, and Melanie Beaton at Coteau Books for all their care and skill.

Edna Alford, Geoffrey Ursell, Luella Newman, Bob Currie, Wenda McArthur, and Larry Warwaruk for comments on the manuscript.

Barbara Frazer, Mike Stiles, Susan Gilmer, Cindy Hamon-Hill, Lyle Johnson, Wayne Schmalz, and the late Kay Sadlemyer for their helpful advice or information.

Thanks to Don Gayton for the insights of *The Wheatgrass Mechanism* and to Melissa Hande and D'Arcy Hande for lending me Kathleen Stokker's book about Norwegian customs in North America. I'm indebted to numerous accounts of myths, in particular Edith Hamilton's *Mythology,* and to

Andrew Nikiforuk's 2004 *Globe and Mail* article on glaciers, and to the documentary film, *Ghengis Blues.*

Thanks to all the Sapergias on the ranch near Old Wives Lake.

The Canada Council for the Arts awarded me a grant which allowed me to complete the first draft of this book, and the Leighton Artists Colony at the Banff Centre provided a wonderful working environment for part of the book. My thanks for this assistance.

Thanks to Geoffrey Ursell for his encouragement and support throughout the writing process, and for all the suppers.

PHOTO: ZACH HAUSER

ABOUT THE AUTHOR

Barbara Sapergia writes fiction and drama for stage, radio, and television. Her first novel, *Foreigners*, told the story of Romanian immigrants in the years before World War I. Her short fiction collection, *South Hill Girls,* was adapted by her for radio and broadcast in Canada by the CBC and on the Australian Broadcasting Corporation. Her second novel, *Secrets in Water,* was nominated for three Saskatchewan Book Awards.

Her eight professionally produced stage plays include *Matty and Rose* (Persephone Theatre), about the struggles of black railway porters to win basic human rights, and *Roundup* (25th Street Theatre), about a prairie ranching family during the droughts of the late 1980s. She is a founder and past president of the Saskatchewan Playwrights Centre. Her radio plays have been aired regionally and on *Morningside, Vanishing Point,* and *Stereodrama.*

Barbara Sapergia has written for the television series *The Way We Are* (CBC), *MythQuest* (CBC, Showcase, PBS), and the children's series she co-created with Geoffrey Ursell, *Prairie Berry Pie* (Global, STN, APTN).

She has lived in Moose Jaw, Regina, Winnipeg, Victoria, Vancouver, and London, England, and now lives in Saskatoon with her husband, writer Geoffrey Ursell.